The STORY of the TIMEPIECE

A COLLECTION OF SHORT STORIES

S. K. POTTEKKAT

Translated from Malayalam by
VENUGOPAL MENON

THORNBIRD
NIYOGI BOOKS

Published by
NIYOGI BOOKS
Block D, Building No. 77,
Okhla Industrial Area, Phase-I,
New Delhi-110 020, INDIA
Tel: 91-11-26816301, 26818960
Email: niyogibooks@gmail.com
Website: www.niyogibooksindia.com

Editor: Jyotika Mansata
Design: Nabanita Das
Cover Design: Jayagovindan Menon

ISBN: 978-93-86906-98-4
Publication: 2019

Printed at: Niyogi Offset Pvt. Ltd., New Delhi, India

Contents

TRANSLATOR'S Note

A Thanksgiving

S.K. Pottekkat—translating him was delightful, because it evoked lingering thoughts and was a learning experience inasmuch as it was therapeutic. Therapeutic because the work of translation puts the mind at rest while stimulating vigorously the creative part of the brain. To highlight just one aspect of the author's style of rendering—it was not until I had completed translating 'Ottakam' (a story in this collection), that I was suddenly besieged with a dull pain of realization of who, in the tale, had sired the infant held so dear by another man even in futile death. Sometimes, it is when you go over the same story again that you experience better, albeit vicariously, the myriad sentiments expounded by the author. Perhaps that is why re-reading some stories can frequently be more delectable than the first time. So it was with me when SKP's stories came my way.

And why did they come my way? I have no one but Mini Krishnan to thank for it. She, with her keen insight and a talent for rearing the obscure to evolve into quality deliverables, asked me to try with a sample she sent. From that point on, she led me by the hand as she walked me through the paces whilst, along the way, I discovered the nuanced world of translation, where verbatim interpretation does not, more often than not, hold water.

Another facet of SKP's style of writing projects his penchant to treat the prosaic almost poetically when he describes landscapes and the behaviour of elements in their natural course. This entails long sentences of illustration whose integrity I have strived to maintain in translation, to convey the mood of the beholder of the scenery; when such portrayal of the verdure written in a native tongue transmutes to another language, the latter cannot altogether bring out and evoke the scents of a place to complete the vicarious experience of an indulgent reader whose sense of smell is inextricably linked to his emotional experiences. A conscious attempt has been made to enhance, similarly, the joy of reading. To cite:

> *Through the crevice between them glisten ice-capped vistas like unopened white umbrellas held aloft. Before us, not far, at the confluence of the Sheshnag River and the snow-bearing Kalahoi River, over the riparian plains of the former, the wooden bridge looking like the skeletal remains of a python, and the river bank covered with smooth stones and wood glitter like a new portrait whose oil paint has not yet lost its wet gloss.* **[Mathruhridayam]**

How much liberty can a translator take? This is debatable. In the portions of his stories where cryptic accounts of characters peek in, the reader, as the translator, will be tempted to draw his own conclusion in interpretation. In the story 'Keechakan', the implied reincarnation of the sister of the eponymous character is cryptic, in that the child bought off a Chinese woman by a stranger in another land, causes a thunderbolt to strike Damu even as he first set eyes on the girl in a different country. But the author teases you with an ending of a tale related to Damu, who then asks Mr Menon, the narrator, if it wasn't a *Chinese woman with a limp* who sold the baby to him in Makassar. Is the answer to this puzzle intriguing but rife with mundane logic? Or was it wishful reincarnation with a chilling explanation to follow?

An uninformed translator might dither here. In this case, the answer comes in the sentence after Damu's query when Menon says: '*That question did not surprise me …*'

A translator must, therefore, read and understand the original script completely before he puts pen to paper, as it were. Clarifications, if needed, must be sought beforehand from the right sources. Each word is chosen with a thought for its origin—a convenient word, clichéd in common parlance, could beget an outright 'No' contextually, if its origin is traced to Latin, Spanish, German, French *et al.* (eg. demeanour, denouement etc.), unless it helped define a character or situation at hand and congruently coalesced with the ambience of the narrative. To cite hypothetically in converse: '*Chirutha could not countenance the ennui of Keeran*' would jar in an otherwise smooth rendition where the context is rustic, or of a lower strata. These and other things were explained to me by Mini Krishnan, who diligently edited all that I produced and gave the stories the sheen that I believe the collection bears in its final form.

I have thoughts of grateful thanks for Dr K. Satchidanandan and Dr M.M. Basheer—the former who, besides advising me on the translation work, also helped in the process of aligning the publisher; and the latter who guided and briefed me on a carefully selected anthology of SKP's stories which he personally took pains to send me. I wish to thank Dr P.P. Raveendran, who agreed to write a Foreword for this work despite the demanding preoccupations of a professor who handles two disciplines in tandem; equally for his open offer to help me during the course of the work so I may avail the benefit of his proficiency in both languages. A line of thanks to Dr Jancy James who volunteered to put together the collection of the chosen stories of SKP in their original form on which the work of translation could commence. But for the earnest help, guidance and motivation of all these personalities mentioned, such a piece of work may not have come to be.

In my few words of thanks, I include here my supportive family, the be all and end all of everything I am … which makes formal thanksgiving appear a little inappropriate (We don't congratulate our mothers on our birthdays, do we?).

Venugopal Menon

Foreword

S.K. Pottekkat: Writing as Fantasy Travel

S.K. Pottekkat (1913–82), the Jnanpith-winning fictionist and travel writer, is one of the few Malayalam authors of his generation whose works embody a steady and consistent evolution. In this, he is different from the common run of writers in most languages who generally belong to one of two categories: one, the class of writers who, in a meteoric rise, demonstrate a flash of creativity early in their careers, produce an outstanding first work and then survive on the basis of that; and two, those who enter the world of writing with an unexceptional first work and then repeat themselves in work after work without any commendable evolution. Pottekkat is different from both these categories in that he represents, in terms of sensibility, a steady growth in his career as a writer, the fruits of which have been put to good use by the fictional tradition in Malayalam continuing from him. He presents the image of a romantic artist in his early writings, and acquires a strong streak of the chronicler of the age as he moves from early literary pieces to his later writings. As a writer of travelogues, he is perhaps a pioneering figure who has laid the foundation for this distinctly modern genre of writing in any Indian language. More importantly, in a metaphorical sense, the idea of travel with the accompanying suggestions of mobility and a concern for the other can be extended to his writing practice in general.

Writing for Pottekkat is surrogate travel, perhaps an act of fantasy travel, which brings the writer and the reader together, and then drives both into contact with new and strange environments. In this sense, Pottekkat is one of the earliest Malayalam litterateurs to internalize the context of what can broadly be described as 'modernity' into his practice of writing, and replicate its form in his evolution as an artist.

Author of 10 novels, 24 short-story collections and 18 travelogues, Pottekkat has also published three verse collections, four plays and a few anthologies of non-fictional prose. He is on record as having stated that the short story is his most favoured medium of creative expression (Jayachandran 1986, 52); his posthumous fame, however, has rested primarily on his fictional masterpiece *Oru Desattinte Katha* (*The Story of a Land*, 1971; trans. as *Tales from Athiranippadam*, 2013), the novel that fetched him the Sahitya Akademi award and the Jnanpith Award. From *Natan Premam* (*Country Love*, 1941) to *Kabeena* (1979), Pottekkat's novels are marked by a progressive engagement with storytelling, an activity that metamorphoses from the record of an individual mind's subjective introspection into a social ritual as one moves from the early novels to the later ones. This is the point in talking about his narrative progress from a romantic artist to a social chronicler. *Oru Desattinte Katha* represents the peak of this narrative journey. The progress here is also from a writer who consciously subscribes to an esoteric aesthetic to one who invalidates that aesthetic by facilitating a textual practice that in essence is non-esoteric. While the early novels like *Natan Premam*, *Moodupadam* (*The Veil*, 1948) and *Vishakanyaka* (*The Fatal Woman*, 1948) are characterized by a concern for an aesthetic that can present the story as an artefact rather than as a narrative practice, the later novels like *Oru Theruvinte Katha* (*A Street's Story*, 1960) and *Oru Desattinte*

Katha appear to be concerned more with telling stories that are also implicated in the dynamics of history and culture.

Indeed, Pottekkat's short stories too participate in this narrative evolution. Of the more than 170 short stories that he has composed during his long creative career, a majority are marked by their social-reformist ardour flavoured with certain distinctively romantic ingredients. In this, his writing seems to echo the general mood of the enhanced social consciousness marking the Indian literary renaissance of the pre-Independence period. His was one of the rare moments in the history of modern Indian literature when the writer made conscious efforts to steer clear of elitism and adopt radical postures associated with the literature of social reform. The emergence of the progressive literary movement in Indian literature was part of this development. This pan-Indian trend flourished in most Indian languages in the pre-Independence days and had some very prominent Indian writers like Munshi Premchand, Saadat Hasan Manto, Faiz Ahmed Faiz, Vijaydan Detha, Habib Tanvir, Amrita Pritam and Mulk Raj Anand subscribing to its ideals. These writers could not escape the romantic ethos that energized their literary response, even as they appealed to the less romantic, down-to-earth aspirations of the commoners. Pottekkat, an activist-nationalist in the pre-Independence days, was an early associate of the progressive literary movement in Malayalam, which also included stalwarts like Vaikom Muhammad Basheer, Thakazhi Sivasankara Pillai, P. Kesava Dev, and Ponkunnam Varkey. The all-pervasive nature of the romantic ambience in the Malayalam literary scenario of the period is further illustrated by the dominant presence of a poet like Changampuzha Krishna Pillai who, though perhaps not as totally committed to the ideals of progressivism as the fictionists mentioned, was seen by the reading public as an icon of the romantic imagination's organic connection with a vision for social reorganization.

Pottekkat's short stories then partake, broadly speaking, of both the romantic idealism and the grand and radical social vision embodied by his novels. His fictional imagination is dominated by myths and fantasies and the magical atmosphere of Indian folk tales on the one hand and the European realist fiction of the nineteenth century on the other. A good many of his stories are set in bizarre and mysterious landscapes across forests, wildernesses and desolate mountain valleys or exotic and outlandish foreign places. Some of the short stories included in the present volume, such as 'Mathruhridayam' (A Mother's Heart), 'Keechakan', 'Pulliman' (Spotted Deer), 'Jeevitam' (Life), 'Kadavu Thoni' (Ferry Boat), and 'Nishagandhi' (Night Queen Flower), bear witness to this. Mysterious human characters involved in weird forms of man-woman relationships set in strange environments are legion in these stories. The man nicknamed 'Ottakam' (literally, the camel) in the story of that title and the *Kirukkan Sayvu* in 'Timepieceinte Katha' (The Story of the Timepiece) are examples. The protagonist of 'Ottakam' gets that name from his physical appearance, which the narrator describes thus: 'Legs like long iron pillars, arms like crowbars and a chest like a china-clay vessel with an elongated neck ... [and] a head like a wilted coconut.' Ottakam is a rustic simpleton, a lonely, half-crazy bachelor employed as a water carrier by the local hotel. His duty is to cart barrels of water from the nearby lake to the hotel, in return for which he is allowed free meals at the hotel. When not on duty, he lives in a world of his own, playing with the village urchins who are his constant companions. One day the roguish hotel manager contrives to get Ottakam to agree to his marriage—only formal and nominal—to Maadhu, the cook, who bears for him a baby six months later, though he has not been allowed to sleep with her for a single night. Ottakam does not bother about not being permitted to live with his wife, but is seen to care deeply for 'his' baby. The story ends on a note of tragic adventurism as Ottakam one day snatches the baby from his wife and hangs himself to death in a room, leaving the baby suspended from his chest.

The Scottish gentleman McCarthy, nicknamed '*Kirukkan Sayvu*'—meaning 'crazy white man'—in 'Timepieceinte Katha' is an equally weird character. He is quite unlike the other Englishmen that the villagers of Wayanad, the setting of the story, in pre-Independence India are familiar with. McCarthy, who has come to India as the manager of a British company, is not like the previous managers of the company who were generally aloof from the local people. He mingles freely with the workers and the local people, who find his antics to be greatly entertaining. It is McCarthy's personal assistant, Kunhikoran butler, who recounts some of these antics to the narrator after McCarthy's return to England. One of these pertain to a beautiful timepiece that adorned McCarthy's drawing-room table. Kunhikoran butler wants the timepiece to be purloined from the absent-minded McCarthy, who is known among his workers as a person given to losing things. The butler knows that it is difficult for a male worker to pass the 'security' check at the gate of McCarthy's bungalow and make off with a pilfered object, and so he arranges for a female worker, Matha, to hide the timepiece in her blouse when she leaves. As luck will have it, the moment Matha passes the gate with the concealed object, the timepiece starts sounding a long alarm and she is caught by the guard on duty. Matha is promptly brought before the *Kirukkan Sayvu* who laughs it off as a joke and lets her go, but summons her again the next day and asks for her hand in marriage.

The plot outlines of the stories 'Ottakam' and 'Timepieceinte Katha' given above shed light on an important aspect of Pottekkat's writing—his narrative interest in incidents and characters. In this, he perhaps deviates from the classic model of the European short story, whose structure is generally characterized by the presence of a discrete and unified experience that is narrated in a compact and focused manner. Very few of Pottekkat's stories follow this classic form. 'Nadeetheerathil' (On the Bank of the River) and 'Upaharam' (The Offering) could perhaps be cited as exceptions to this. Most of his other stories present everyday incidents with detailed descriptions of the environment and the background setting drawn on vast canvases as well as characters who appear to resemble real-life people one meets in everyday life. There is a pronounced predisposition for realistic narration in Pottekkat's creative personality, his romantic sensibility notwithstanding. He was always inclined towards the drab, the banal and the routine, and this inclination can be seen to become an obsession with him in some of his later works, especially in the novel *Oru Desattinte Katha*. His prototype for fiction writing, he has indicated in some of his interviews, is the series of letters that he, as a young boy, was asked to write on behalf of the unlettered woman in the neighbourhood to her husband living away from her. Truthfulness to day-to-day experiences is an important aspect of his creative practice. He once estimated the proportion of truth and fantasy in his fiction to be 80:20, which, he was quick to emphasise, had no chance of ever being reversed (Basheer 2013, 11). He was in the habit of keeping a writer's notebook, in which he recorded his impressions on the quotidian world and the experiences he acquired in his interaction with men and matters. He was also in the habit of pouring his thoughts and feelings into his diary (Jayachandran 1986, 53).

To return to the point made regarding his connection with modernity, Pottekkat is one of the few writers of his generation who provides a clear model of a third-world artist whose work is complicated by the contradictory pulls of modernity. His romantic worldview, his affinity with realism, his concern for the everyday, his interest in formal aesthetics, and the colonialist biases sometimes displayed in his attitude to the denizens of the non-European world, are all certainly aspects of modernity. Each of these characteristics is to be examined in detail in order to make a proper evaluation of Pottekkat as an artist. In our analysis of 'Ottakam' and 'Timepieceinte Katha', we have already seen the way in which he works an attitude to the real into the form of his fiction. He can be seen to put his penchant for realism to good use in his later writings, especially in *Oru Desattinte Katha*, which can be described as a Bakhtinian dialogical novel that looks askance at his own early romanticism. The passage from the romantic to the Bakhtinian, in the case of Pottekkat, seems to have been a smooth one, and is not intercut, as is the case with some of his younger contemporaries, with a phase of modernism. Pottekkat does not seem to have been favourably disposed to the formalist experiments connected with the literary modernism of the 1960's, but he could not have been unresponsive to the increasing obsolescence of the romantic worldview that his early short stories and novels such as 'Pulliman' and *Vishakanyaka* embodied. In a 1979 interview, Pottekkat acknowledges his difficulty with the language of the modernists, but recognizes at the same time that sensibilities have changed. 'Changes can be seen in ideas, philosophies and ways of expression,' he says, and adds: 'There is a total change in forms and themes. Fiction is now infected by the new energy transmitted by science and technology, by politics and journalism' (Pottekkat 2013a, 66).

The voice of the romantic artist, however, is very strong in Pottekkat's early writings, and it was perhaps as a romantic writer that he constructed his own self-image. There is a reference in one of his travelogues, *London Notebook* (1970), to a meeting he had in London with V.K. Krishna Menon, India's Malayalam-speaking High Commissioner to the UK in the early 1950's, to whom Pottekkat introduces himself with some pride as a writer of romantic fiction (Pottekkat 2001, 28). While his romantic worldview indeed drove him to compose some of his classic stories like 'Pulliman' and 'Nadeetheerathil', it also seems to have imparted to him a certain colonialist bias in his attitude to Africans and other members of the non-European world. In his travelogues, he would invariably refer to the native African as an uncivilized '*kappiri*' (from the Arabic word 'kafir', meaning 'an infidel'; the English equivalent would be 'nigger'), a 'primitive' being who can only look upon a person from the 'civilized' world with awe and wonder. *Kappirikalude Naattil* (*In the Land of the Negro*, 1951), it is significant to remember, is the title of his travel writing on Africa. Describing the puzzled expression on the face of a black African at the port watching the approaching ship, Pottekkat says: 'He must have cast the same look of wonder at Vasco da Gama's ship when it anchored off the coast of Africa in 1497. The wonder in his eyes remains unchanged even after centuries. That precisely is the reason why there is no progress for him' (Pottekkat 2003, 13). The argument is not substantially different from the Euro-centric argument proffered by the colonizer in his criticism of the 'primitive' state of affairs in India and other colonies. Most colonial scholars thought that things remained unchanged for centuries before the arrival of the British in India and other parts of the colonized world, and that was why they considered it their moral duty—the white man's burden—to launch their civilizing mission in the colonies.

Pottekkat echoes this colonialist bias in the depiction of black Africans in his travel writings, but appears to take a different position in his short stories. Look at the short story titled 'Quahe-ri' (Farewell), which provides a sketch of the Englishman, Sally, son of a rich British planter from Kenya, who falls in love with Africa and befriends the local people. His research on African dance takes him to the heartland of African village life, which allows him to discover the shades in the emotional experience of the African blacks and meld with the core of African folk culture. His proximity to the natives distances him from members of his own community settled in Africa. Sally is opposed to the arrogant and violent ways of the Englishmen in their dealings with the Africans and wants his countrymen to treat the natives with love and respect. 'Let no Englishman hope in vain to take the land of Africa by force, a land that was once conquered by love by the missionary Livingstone,' he used to say. In fact, he demonstrates his love for the natives by marrying a black African woman named Kabeena, who had saved him earlier from an attempt on his life hatched by some degenerate natives. The story ends on a disquieting note as reports arrive of Sally being shot dead by a fellow Britisher. 'Quahe-ri' in the title is the native expression for 'farewell' which is repeated in several contexts of leave-taking narrated in the text—Sally taking leave of the narrator after the two meet in the compartment of a train; Kabeena taking leave of Sally after the latter resolves to quit the village in the face of the threat on his life—but assumes a new meaning when it appears at the end of the story as a final farewell to Sally.

The element of realism that appears in 'Avalude Keralam' (Her Keralam) too is an integral part of Pottekkat's narrative art. This story, which is set in Malaysia and is presented as a fictional cogitation on the question of national identity, has the Indian Union's reorganization, post-Independence, into states on the basis of linguistic affiliation in 1956 as its context. Kerala, which till then had remained divided as the three separate regions of Travancore, Cochin and Malabar, is now united and turns into a constituent state of the Indian Union. This is the 'new Kerala' that the newspapers of the day are vocal about. But the phrase intrigues the teenager Prabha, a girl born to Chinese parents, but brought up as the daughter of a Malayali engineer working in Malaysia. Prabha has always considered Kerala to be her homeland, and is now greatly puzzled to see the map of a 'new' Kerala printed in a weekly. What is this new Kerala? Is there an 'old' Kerala as well? 'From the earliest days she could remember, the Kerala that dwelt in her mind was just one. Was it losing its identity?' she wonders. There is a clear indication in the story that a nation is built in fantasy and imagination, in the language that the people speak, in their memories and in the tales and stories that they narrate. Prabha, with an adopted national identity, has no problem, emotional or intellectual, in imagining herself to be a Malayali. A girl who avidly follows the literature of Kerala, she often exchanges books with her Malayali friends. A few Malayalam books would keep her engaged for weeks together. 'She knew by heart the old rustic literary works of Kerala, like *Harinamakeertanam, Sheelavati, Bheemankatha, Seethadukkham* etc., and also tribal songs like *Kurathipattu.* Achan had taught her the nuances of the tunes and the typical way these songs were to be sung.' Composed years before Benedict Anderson (1983) came up with his influential thesis on the nation as an imagined community, Pottekkat's 'Avalude Keralam' can be described as a provocative text that raises significant questions about the interplay of reality and illusion in the construction of the nation.

'Avalude Keralam' also embodies Pottekkat's creative attempt at making sense of certain unknown segments of the writer's self, a self that is contiguous with the physical terrain, and which finds its final flowering in *Oru Desattinte Katha.* Construction of the self indeed is one of the important ways in which the modern individual gets engendered in the real world. Fiction in the present-day world, after all, is a means of constructing the individual self through explorations into landscapes of the mind, which open out into the larger avenues of the outer world's geography. The only ethical reason for fiction's existence, according to the German novelist Hermann Broch, is its ability to reveal 'a hitherto unknown segment of existence' (quoted in Kundera 1988, 5). As for Pottekkat the writer of travel, both real and fantasy, his short stories are redolent with the smell not just of one unknown segment of existence, but of countless segments, which may still not add up to the image of a well-plotted geography wherein one proposes to travel. Whether the travel is real or fantasy, these narratives are connected to a deeply fragmented world of experience. Perhaps Pottekkat makes a virtue of the world's fragmented nature, so that each trip would be a new experience for the reader. These tales also demonstrate that Pottekkat is a successful storyteller, whose stories initiate a pedagogic reconstruction of the collective memory of a people. It was Walter Benjamin who suggested, famously, that storytelling, an activity close to the cultural practice of oral narration, leads invariably to 'the transmission of a moral message' (Benjamin 1973, 87). Pottekkat's stories realize the transmission of such a message by turning his texts into sites of textual and cultural practice. The textual practice that Pottekkat initiates through his fiction corresponds to Benjamin's storytelling that brings into being a community of readers who would actively body forth a collective subject and a collective history in the process of reading the story. It is to this correspondence that most of Pottekkat's mature fiction, including 'Quahe-ri', 'Avalude Keralam', and *Oru Desattinte Katha,* point ultimately.

P.P. Raveendran

WORKS CITED

Anderson, Benedict. 1983. *Imagined Communities: The Origin and Spread of Nationalism*. London: Verso.

Basheer, M.M. 2013. 'Njaanariyunna SK.' *Granthalokam* 63.4: 7-12.

Benjamin, Walter. 1973. *Illuminations.* Trans. Harry Zohn. London: Fontana.

Jayachandran, T.N. 1986. *Kathayude Pinnile Katha*. Kottayam: SPCS.

Kundera, Milan. 1988. *The Art of the Novel.* Trans. Linda Asher. London: Faber.

Pottekkat, S.K. 1971. *Oru Desattinte Katha.* Kottayam: SPCS.

----------. 2001. *London Notebook.* Kottayam: DC Books.

----------. 2003. *Sanchara Sahityam Sampoornam*. Kottayam: DC Books.

----------. 2013a. *Kabeena*. Kozhikode: Mathrubhumi.

----------. 2013b. *Tales from Athiranippadam*. Trans. Sreedevi K. Nair and Radhika P. Menon. Hyderabad: Orient BlackSwan.

Camel
Ottakam

Everyone called him Ottakam.

Legs like long iron pillars, arms like crowbars and a chest like a *cheenabharani* with an elongated neck—on the top of this aggregate, a head like a wilted coconut! That was Ottakam.

Ottakam, towing a *peepavandi* filled with water, trudging through the streets both in the morning and again in the evening, was a sight to behold. Trailing that cart, which rode on four small squeaky wheels emitting a jarring note and crawling like a pig in labour, would be a few urchins pretending to push the cart helpfully from behind. Some of them would be quarrelling, making faces at each other and grumbling as they walked along. Some would turn their necks to watch the amusements of the street and grin, baring their teeth in glee. All of them moved after the cart, pointing to it, without actually touching it. Ottakam was totally unaware of all this. The man would continue to strain forward, both his arms tangled and knotted around the metal hooks of the cart, head held high and lips clasped tightly shut. Once in a while, he would stick out his lower lip, pucker his nose and look at either side of the road. It was that contorted glance of his that had earned him the name, 'Ottakam'.

He wore an old, foul-smelling length of linen once used on the dining table of the hotel. Besides this was a piece of cloth tied around his right calf. It was the memento of a bruise suffered long ago. The bruise had healed and dried and hair had grown over new skin, but he continued to keep that piece of cloth wrapped around his calf. He must have thought that if that piece of cloth came undone, he would instantly roll over and die. He went around wearing it on his leg like a badge of honour.

His resting place was a spot next to a bin of leavings adjacent to the firewood shed. In the evenings he would sit there craning his neck, his torso erect, smoking a cheroot. His helpers, the urchins, would clamber all over his back and shoulders in play. For him it was just a pastime. After a long while he would suddenly jump to his feet. The children would tumble to the ground like so many puppies at which he would burst into raucous laughter like the braying of a donkey.

Ottakam and the urchins lived as dependents of that big hotel. His job, which he had been doing for 16 years, was to fetch all the water the hotel needed from the lake nearby in the barrel-mounted cart. Nobody knew anything about his life before this span of 16 years. Nobody had enquired, either. It was now impossible to envisage him as anything other than an integral part of that barrel wagon.

This way, he lived on.

'A fellow, who at one sitting eats a quantity meant for eight!' is the only complaint the hotel manager had against Ottakam. Besides hauling the water to the hotel, he also performed the chore of chopping firewood. India became tumultous with the August revolt, the Second World War ended and the country became an independent nation. Ottakam was not aware of all this. Only on two occasions did he realize that there were unusual things happening in a world unknown to him.

One morning, as usual, when he was hauling the water cart to the hotel, there was picketing at the gates of a factory by the wayside. Suddenly, a lorry load of policemen arrived and 'lathi-charged' all the picketers and the bystanders. Ottakam, tugging his cart, was caught in the midst of all this commotion. He dropped the cart and ran. A blow struck his back as he ran. He pressed both his hands to his back and, wrinkling his nose and sticking out his neck and lower lip, ran helter-skelter without looking back. He would not stop even when he reached his street. He looked at the shopkeepers on either side of the road and splitting his mouth, forming a hollow like a cave, still running, he cautioned them in a suppressed tone, 'The cane is behind us!'

It was his firm belief that everyone was about to get their backsides caned.

The whole day, Ottakam remained seated in the firewood shed, wincing. In spite of the advice and scolding of the hotel manager, he would not budge. Finally the urchins somehow hauled that *peepavandi* from where he had left it and brought it to the hotel. It was only on that day that the children experienced the actual weight of that loaded barrel cart.

The second instance was when that cart toppled and fell on his back. That simpleton must have attained salvation in that very instant. With his skull and backside crushed and bathed in blood, Ottakam extricated himself from beneath the barrel. He slithered a short distance and collapsed there. The hotel manager arranged for him to be taken to a hospital in a rickshaw. Everybody thought Ottakam would breathe his last. He was that badly broken and crushed. But survive he did.

When Ottakam regained consciousness, he found himself lying on a smooth white mattress. He surveyed his whole body. His head, jaw and shoulders were all tightly bound with strips of white cloth. Glancing at his right calf, he found that old strip of cloth missing. He immediately ripped off the cloth from his head and bandaged his calf securely with it, and lay back satisfied, eyes closed. When the nurse came a little later to check on him, he was seen with a thick trickle of blood oozing from his head and was unconscious again. He remained in the hospital for a month and a half on a cot in a corner of the verandah.

One night, when the doctor on duty went to check a noise coming from the verandah, he saw Ottakam moving on the verandah, towing that iron cot after him. He was compensating for the distress he felt for not being able to draw his *peepavandi.*

Ottakam was discharged from the hospital the very next day. As soon as he reached the hotel, he tugged his barrel cart and set out towards the lake.

One day, the hotel manager sent for him. Ottakam was bewildered. Not knowing what was about to transpire, he stood there sniffing with his face raised, wrinkling his nose and lips. Finally, extending his neck as far as it would go in a show of submission and great respect, he presented himself before the manager.

The manager looked him over head to toe and said: 'Hey you! I called to tell you something. How old are you now?'

Ottakam stood there gaping.

'You may not know. Never mind. Since you have worked for this hotel for a very long time I feel a special affection for you. Therefore, I have decided to arrange a wedding for you. What do you say?'

Ottakam blanched and froze.

'She is a good girl—do you know who? It is Maadhu who works in the kitchen. As you are both my employees you do not have to gift her anything in particular. As for the wedding expenses ...'

The manager opened the drawer of his table and extracted three ten-rupee notes from a bunch stacked inside a tin of cigarettes and placed them on the table.

'There is an amount here that is due to you as salary. I shall make up for whatever falls short, as my gift. Do you agree, or what?'

Ottakam stood there gaping, unable to answer. It was his belief till then that subjects like girls, weddings did not affect him and were matters that he had no right of claim to. The manager's announcement stirred awake a tingle in his shrivelled nerve centers. Ottakam puckered his nose and mouth awry, looked at either side of the room, sniffing.

'You have to answer me soon. Do you agree?' the manager asked in a grave tone, his voice slightly raised.

Ottakam bared his teeth and rocked his head from side to side in a gesture of consent.

'Then you may leave. Tomorrow night is your wedding. You need not fetch water or chop wood tomorrow.'

Very slowly, Ottakam descended the staircase and reached the back of the hotel. After a while he called the urchins one by one and whispered in their ears: 'Tomorrow is my wedding!'

None of them believed him at first.

'What wedding? A *kurikalyanam*?'

That evening the hotel manager summoned him and gifted him a shirt, a double dhoti and a *veshti*. When they saw the new dresses for the groom, the brats realized what Ottakam had said was true. They climbed onto his back and asked, 'Who is the girl?'

'You can see her tomorrow.' Ottakam said with gravity.

Night fell the next day. The rush in the hotel subsided and everything became peaceful. All the arrangements for the wedding had been made in room number 10. Wearing the new clothes, Ottakam entered the room, a little nervously. The bandage on his calf was just where it always was. The bride was seated on a reed mat, all decked up. Ottakam glanced at her. He realized instantly that the plump woman with a complexion of rice bran was indeed Maadhu, the kitchen maid. Suppressing his beastly glee he stood rooted, gaping at her.

The rituals of the wedding were completed in the presence of and with the help of the manager and a few of his friends. The children were not allowed entry. All they could do was climb onto the roof of the firewood shed and watch from there. Despite the night being brightly moonlit, it drizzled abruptly.

'*Rain and shine for the fox's wedding;*

Rain and moonlight for the camel's wedding!'

Shouting in verse accompanied by a burst of laughter, the children climbed down from their perch and went to bed. Once the wedding was over, Ottakam stood there gawking, not knowing what to do next. The manager ordered him to go back to his usual place to sleep. A little later, the bridegroom lay asleep surrounded by urchins.

Ottakam went on living as usual, without understanding what he had gained or otherwise lost. Marriage was one of the many things that he could not understand in life.

Months passed.

Although there was no change in him apparently, thoughts gnawed at his brain. Whereas he was seldom afflicted by illness, a severe headache now troubled him. There was no longer the sniffing looks at the street when he drew the barrel cart. His neck shrank and head bowed. He would lose his temper unreasonably and then he would roar in a crackling voice.

He saw Maadhu at times. He would glance at her while she grated coconuts and fried masala in the kitchen. He got his chance that day when he was filling water in the tank beside the well in the kitchen. Whenever she saw Ottakam she would giggle, covering her mouth with her hands, quaking all over.

He endured everything.

After six months of the wedding, Ottakam heard that Maadhu had given birth to a healthy male child.

One day, he was going along tugging his cart with its barrel of water.

Suddenly, the brats yelled: 'Ottakam's child!'

Ottakam turned his neck to look. Maadhu was walking along the side of the street. Held against her bosom was an infant. Ottakam's eyes lit up. He smiled beautifully like an ordinary person, stopped his cart and walked up to Maadhu. Maadhu stood transfixed. Ottakam gathered that tender infant from her hip and, tucking it under his arm, began to walk back to his cart. He began to move ahead, holding the baby tightly under one arm and drawing the cart with the other.

Maadhu ran after the cart hollering. The children hooted. A crowd gathered. Hearing all this uproar, a policeman too reached there.

The minute Ottakam glimpsed the policeman he dropped his cart and vamoosed. He wondered where he could run to. He was unable to think of any other place but the premises of the hotel. Holding the child tightly under his arm, he hurtled towards the hotel. When he noticed the presence of a policeman there too, he ran up to the top floor of the hotel in fright. That old room number 10 was lying open. He got in and closed the door after him.

The hotel manager, Maadhu, the policemen and a small group of people gathered in front of the room.

'Hey you! Open the door!' the manager ordered. No response.

Pounding on the door he shouted once more: 'You better open the door, good and proper, I tell you!'

'I will not part with the child!' Ottakam said in a mournful wail from within.

'We will talk about it later. You open the door and come out right now.'

'This child is for me.' That melancholy voice came again from inside the room.

'I told you to open the door!' The manager hammered on the door with force.

'I did not get the mother. I must have the child.' Ottakam pleaded pathetically.

'What is he saying? Whose child is this?' asked the policeman.

'It is her child.' The manager said without paying attention.

'That I understood. Who is the father of the infant?'

Ignoring the query of the policeman, the manager shouted to the man inside the room: 'What are you going to do to the child?'

'I will bring it up alone, or sell it or even kill it. This is my child,' replied Ottakam.

'Aha! So you have come to that! If you don't open the door I will kick open the door and kill you!'

'If you pound the door again, I will throw the baby out through the window. Hmm ...!' Ottkam warned them in a queer voice.

'Oh my God! That creature will kill the child!' Maadhu wailed in a semi-conscious state.

'*Kunji, bavo, bavo* ...' They heard Ottakam's lullaby from inside the room.

The manager was in a predicament. Some in the crowd lingered anxiously, not knowing what would happen next. Some found it a delightful pastime. The policeman made as if to go downstairs implying, 'This is a civil case, not criminal; I have no role here.'

The manager stopped him. 'When a murder is about to take place here, are you leaving as if you are not aware of all this?' he asked him in a grave tone.

'It is enough if you call me when it is done. Till then I have nothing to do here.' Saying so much, the policeman walked down the stairs with a grave face.

The manager was perplexed, not knowing what to do. If the door was broken open and Ottakam threw the child down to the street as he had threatened, the matter would become calamitous. The shrill scream of the child was heard again. There was no way of knowing if Ottakam was fondling the child or killing it.

'Listen! We will give the child to you. It will cry itself to death. You open the door. We will not do anything.' The manager tried speaking in a calm tone.

No response.

The cry of the child could be heard continuously.

'Let him remain closed in there. He will jump out when he gets hungry,' said one of the spectators.

'What about loosening the tiles on the roof and quietly getting inside?' suggested another.

'Even before they jump inside, that animal will finish them off,' the manager warned in a firm voice. 'Let us see how many days he remains like that.'

'Let anything happen to him; but that baby—won't it die of starvation?' said Kanaran, the agent of the hotel.

'Anyway, let us wait for daybreak. By then it is unlikely that his mood will not change.'

Deciding thus, the manager and his friends left the place. Agent Kanaran slept outside the door as guard. Next morning the manager and his buddies went up to room number 10 and began to call out.

Silence from within.

Finally, they decided to break open the door and enter. They smashed the door and peeped inside. Hanging from the rafter was the naked corpse of Ottakam! On his bosom lay the infant. He had removed the old cloth that he wore and with it bound the baby safely to his chest. He had tied the bed sheet to the rafter and hanged himself.

The manager climbed on top of the almirah and unwound the cloth and took the baby from the chest of the dead man. The body of the child had not turned cold yet. Its heart was beating feebly. 'The child is not dead! The child is not dead!' Bellowing, the manager and his group ran outside.

With that long neck, twisted tongue sticking out and eyes half shut, the naked lifeless body of Ottakam, assisted by a light breeze that wafted in through the window, swirled slowly around—and gazed at that infant.

A Mother's Heart

Mathruhridayam

The evening seemed to be preparing for snowfall. The piercing wind that came caressing the icy stalagmite of the Kalahoi blew over and over again.

We stood gripping the iron grill of the balcony of the room we had rented in Kashmir Hotel in Pahalgam, all too afraid to venture outside, staring idly at the deep forest in the distance.

Towering hills, wearing pine trees like a pleated green skirt and snowflakes like a *parda,* stood confounding direction like Pathan dancers with their backs turned. Through the crevice between them glistened ice-capped vistas like unopened white umbrellas held aloft. Before us, not far, at the confluence of the Sheshnag River and the snow-bearing Kalahoi River, over the riparian plains of the former, the wooden bridge—looking like the skeletal remains of a python—and the river bank, covered with smooth stones and wood, glittered like a new portrait whose oil paint has not yet lost its wet gloss. The mist prowling across the river moved steadily forward smoking, as it were, the light of day. On the lawn below the hotel, a European family had pitched tent below a big deodar tree. Before the tent sat a European lady on a cane chair, sipping hot coffee. Beside her near the river, a couple of European children aged six and seven were playing, filling pebbles in colourful wicker baskets.

Abruptly, the children began to wail and call out. A butler in a white turban leapt out of the tent and began to pelt stones: 'Shoo, shoo!'

That is when I first saw her. An old Muslim woman, of about fifty was running scared, supporting herself with a stick. Somehow she caught hold of the side rail of that wood bridge. Swinging her stick, she hurriedly crossed the bridge to the safety of the other side. She stood still, holding the abutment of the bridge, listening to the shouts and yells of the children.

I did not understand anything. All of a sudden, Karan Singh, the manager of the hotel came upstairs to ask about the dishes we wanted for dinner.

Pointing to that old woman I asked, 'Is she a beggar?'

'No.' He shook his head.

'Insane?'

'No.'

Then he cast a smile and said, 'In a manner of speaking, it wouldn't be wrong to call Rehti a beggar or insane.'

'Who is she?' I asked again. 'Why did the butler shoo her away?'

'She is a being that always lingers around the tents of Europeans.'

'With what intent? To beg for food, perhaps?'

'No. The children of the white folks are the objects of her attraction.'

'The delight of seeing them, isn't it?'

'She cannot see. Rehti is blind. She comes to listen to the loud chatter of the children. If she gets the chance, she will hug them close to her chest, kiss their cheeks and scurry away. Only white children.

'What is the reason for this abnormal behavior?'

'To understand that you have to hear the whole story of Rehti, Babuji,' Karan Singh said, stroking his beard. 'What shall I prepare for dinner? Fowl fry, khorma, omelette?' He reminded us of the dishes on his menu. But more than those items of food, what I preferred, for the time being, was to hear the life story of that old woman who trailed after white children.

I had to be patient till dinner was through. After dinner we waited in our room. When it was past eight, Karan Singh came, having finished all his work in the hotel, hauling a large hookah, and sat before us.

Transcribed below is the story he told us.

'About 50 years ago in the quiet of the winter of Kashmir she was born, seeing only the glow of darkness, as the blind daughter of a goatherd, in a bamboo hut in the village of Maimal situated about four or five miles above the Sheshnag River—just think of it, Babuji! To be born blind in this *aniyara* of beauty and colour! How cruel must the Creator be to send Rehti blindfolded to this lively refuge of such beauty from where Paradise appears to be a mere shouting distance away!

Leaving behind her blind infant in this world, the mother passed on. Her father brought her up with the help of an old woman. Years passed. But Rehti was not aware of the loss that she had inherited at birth. She grew up in a magical world of her own.

The quintessence of life in Kashmir blessed her. She lived in a world of sounds, glided with fragrances. Her thoughts assumed colours. She learned the songs of the birds of the forest. She could tell the birds apart from the sound of the flapping of their wings. When the breeze blew gently, she could tell one tree from another by the rustling of the leaves. She recognized that each forest rivulet had a distinct musical strain of its own. By the turbulence in the flow of air, her keen enthusiasm and a mysterious blessing of conscience, she could predict the changes in weather and the fluctuating moods of the atmosphere.

She walked carefree around the forest hooting, mimicking the birds of the wilderness. She also helped graze the goats of her *bappa*. 'Hoi! Hoi! Hoi!'—her cry to flock the goats together rang out in the forest. She would gather firewood, make bundles and carry them on her head to their hut, and sit on the bank of the stream and catch fish with a rod and line. She could cook too. But there was one thing that she was not aware of—that she was growing to be the most beautiful young woman in Kashmir.

As a woman she did not know much about herself. Once she heard an opinion from a youth. She had gone to the forest to gather firewood with Sainuddin, the naughty son of Mahmood, the horse tender. Having bundled the firewood, they sat under a deodar tree to rest awhile. The birds of the forest were warbling, perched on the branches of trees. Suddenly, Sainuddin caught her hand and said: '*Rehti, sooshchekh badsondarkoor.*' (Rehti, you are a very beautiful girl).

She split her blind eyes wide open and asked: 'Sainu, whoever said that?'

'Everyone says so. The shepherd Gulam Hussan, Mahmud chacha, the horse tender Abdulla, Sardar who runs the hotel—all of them say so. '*Rehti badsondar*!'

After remaining silent for some time, she asked: 'Sainu, what is it that they call beautiful? What is special about me that is different from other girls?'

'When you walk past, everybody gawks at you.'

'That is because I am blind.'

'No. They say that such a beauty as you has not been born in Kashmir before. That you are a *hoorling.* I have heard the post office babu tell the scrap vendor Kasim that Rehti's cheeks are made of apples, her eyes the black berries of rose-apple trees, her mouth of pomegranates and that her body is made of wild roses and her breasts peaked heaps of snow; God has created Rehti using the pristine natural riches of Kashmir.'

Rehti sat lost in thought staring upward. Still she could not understand. She asked again: 'What is this thing called beauty?'

Sainuddin could not explain it to her in words. An idea struck him. Saying, 'Men would want to do this when they see you!' that mischievous boy planted a kiss on Rehti's cheek.

In the same instant, Rehti gave Sainuddin's cheek a tight slap. Sainuddin laughed uproariously and stepping away, called out from afar: 'Oh, flower of Kashmir, when the man who marries you too does this, will you slap him? Ha! Ha! Ha! But that will not happen. Who will ever marry a blind girl?'

Rehti turned seventeen. It was the month of March. Rain and sleet withdrew. More than anyone else, Rehti experienced the gradual blossoming of spring in the pulse of the atmosphere and the thrilling stirrings of vernal life, the fragrance and the rays of golden light. With the onset of spring Pahalgam came alive. The hotels opened. The tourists pitched their tents beneath the canopied tops of chinar trees.

Rehti's father had become an old man and, no longer able to go to work, spent his days in the hut. Old age and rheumatism had frozen him. Poverty enveloped that hut. Concern for his daughter pained him evenly through night and day. Of what use was her extraordinary beauty? No man in that forest village would marry her. They would prefer a toiling female monster who worked in farms to a blind celestial nymph.

As the old man spent his days in anxiety and sorrow over what would happen to his daughter when he was gone, one day, the horse tender of Pahalgam, Rasheed walked into his house. The old man received Rasheed courteously. Both of them smoked the hookah and talked of local matters.

Rasheed was around forty-five years old. He had to call his own, three ponies, three regular wives and a limp. Confronted with his narrow, flattened yellow face with its mixed Mongolian features and two deep-set eyes that looked like screws driven into sockets, an ugly mustache with its ends turned down in a slant and his deceptive smile—there was no one who wouldn't feel a sense of apprehension at that moment.

'Grandpa, haven't you become old?' he asked aloud, puffing out smoke from the hookah.

'Hmm ...'

'What will happen to Rehti?'

The old man did not say anything.

'I am thinking of marrying Rehti,' Rashid said, blowing out a puff of smoke.

The old man who was partially deaf did not hear very well what was said.

'Huh?' The old man gaped at Rashid's face.

'I am thinking of marrying Rehti.' Rashid leaned over to the old man and shouted in his ear.

Rehti, who was standing holding the bamboo door of the kitchen, stepped back a little, startled by those words. Marriage? It was a word that evoked in her an unknown fear similar to that of death. She did not know what the love of a man was. Although at the commencement of spring she would experience a magical emotion of mild warmth touch her nerves, she had never known the romantic, sensual touch of a man's flesh.

The conversation outside continued.

'Don't you know that Rehti is blind?'

'Bapu! That does not matter. I want her. I have two wives to do the household chores and work in the farm. I merely want to go on seeing Rehti as the queen of my house,' said Rashid.

The old man felt as if a heavy burden was sliding and falling off his life. He heaved a sigh and said: 'I would be happy.'

Inside, Rehti cringed. The old man and Rashid went on talking for a long time, smoking the hookah. What if Rehti could have seen Rashid frequently looking inwards triumphantly, flashing that dirty smile!

As soon as Rashid bade farewell and left, Rehti fell into the lap of the old man sobbing: 'I am not going away with anyone. I shall stay on here. I don't want him. His speech is foul. I felt the dirty stench of liquor coming from his mouth.'

'My darling child,' the old man said, stroking the top of her head, 'You do not know anything about life. When my time is over, you will freeze and decay like the flowering creepers in winter. The only good fortune in your life is this marriage. Rashid is a man with verve. Accept *Bappa*'s advice!'

Droplets of tears from the old man's eyes dripped onto Rehti's forehead. Thereon, that wedding too took place. Rashid took his fresh bride to an isolated grass hut in one corner of Pahalgam. He engaged an old woman as a help for Rehti.

Rehti did tell me once, the story of her married life in a touchingly frank manner. Even from the nuptial night, Rehti despised Rashid. Rashid too had married that blind girl with a specific intention. 'Rehti must hate me!' That was what he wanted.

In the month of May, the white tourists began to arrive regularly in Pahalgam. Two weeks after the marriage of his daughter, the old man died.

One evening Rashid came to her and said: 'Tonight, I am going to Astham Marg as a guide for a mountaineering party. A master of mine, a white man, will come here tonight. You must behave meekly with him.'

That night she experienced the odour of a strange man in her bed. She could not understand his language. She had already become familiar with the foul smell of liquor. The passionate hot touch of the white man and his antics in bed aroused her to a new world. That fawn, wounded by the repulsive beastly attacks of Rashid, dissolved in ecstasy.

He asked several questions which she could not understand. His pronunciation sounded like the bubbling of boiling water. Smiling, she stroked his whole face, tentatively. A nose like an *ettameen.* A long moustache like a hairy caterpillar wrapped around his upper lip. Hair like curls of silk threads ... Rehti liked that white man.

Two days passed. Rashid brought a new guest. She felt she was being crushed by a mountain of flesh. A monster. But he too had the same smell as the white man. She liked that smell. On another occasion, Rashid got her dressed up and took her to a tent. She does not know how many people ravaged her. She returned to her hut leaning on Rashid, her clothes stained with blood.

She lived on this way. That virtuous girl, who once gleamed with the purity of driven snow and the freshness of a flower, lived suffocating in the drain overflowing with the toxic sewage of prostitution. With the profit earned from his new arrangement, Rashid bought two more ponies.

Rehti became pregnant. Beneath the fear and the revulsion, it was not that she did not have a secret sensation of joy. By the month of October, the visitors departed and she gained respite. At the onset of the next spring season she gave birth to a male child. The first cry of that child caused a tickle in her life. She held that warm mass of flesh close to her bosom. Let the father be anyone. Isn't it her own child, the child born of her womb? The mother lay hugging her 'treasure' close to her bosom.

A week passed. Rashid walked in one day and examined the child. 'This won't do here,' he commanded. 'This child which looks like a white leaf with eyes and hair the colour of rice bran—nobody will believe the child is of a Kashmiri.' He wrenched the child off her bosom and walked out.

Rehti lay there, unconscious.

He had decided to throw the child into the ice-laden river from the top of an icy hillock. But as he climbed the hill, an idea occurred to him. One or two European families had arrived at Pahalgam as soon as the spring season set in. He turned back and walked towards their tents. He approached a European lady and said: 'I have found a child below a tree over there!' They were surprised to see the fair child whom Rashid was holding up in his hands like a toy. He sold the baby for Rs.15. With that money he bought himself a fur coat.

The month of June arrived. Pahalgam filled up with visitors. There were many white folks too. Rashid resumed his arrangement. Rehti became pregnant again. The child she gave birth to did not cry. 'Is this also a white child?' she asked the old helper woman. It was a girl child the colour of rice bran. But it was lifeless. Cursing Rehti, Rashid threw it into the snow.

Spring seasons came and passed. Rehti delivered four more babies. Like bread straight out of the oven, Rashid sold each of them to white people, right away. Nine years passed. Rehti gave birth to a final child—also lifeless. The same year Rashid breathed his last. On an occasion when he had accompanied a group of mountaineers to climb an icy peak, a large boulder of ice slid down upon him, squashing him to death.

Rehti had become an ugly woman, having lost the glow of her body afflicted by sexually transmitted diseases and premature aging. But her passion for life did not perish. She still resides in that very hut.

A futile hope that children born of her might be somewhere in the tents of the white men is what draws her towards these tents. Poor thing! That mother does not know that years have gone by. Her children might now be studying in Oxford University in England or elsewhere. Or they could be somewhere in Hindustan as ICS officers. With a heart throbbing with longing, that old woman stays put here awaiting the white tourists of the spring season. If she could get to pet those white children, it would be for her, salvation. But everybody knows her tale. The minute they see her shadow, the servants of the white folks pelt stones and chase her away.

That is the story of Rehti's life.'

When I heard the story of Rehti the sensation in my heart was not unlike the one I experienced when I ventured a dip in the gelid waters of the river in Pahalgam, that morning.

Keechakan

I was a guest for a day in Jakarta. I stayed in the multi-storied building of a textile shop in 'Pasar Baru', the large market of Jakarta. My host was Mr Menon. He and his Eurasian wife lived in a portion of an old godown at the eastern end of the building. Menon had arranged a small room at the western end of the building for me that night. As there was no electric lamp in that room we entered the room with a small candle.

The stench of stale air pervaded the room; probably because it had been kept locked for a very long time. There were not too many things in it. An old cot, an old mat on it that looked like the skin of a python and a pillow that resembled a bandicoot. A small, square wicker table and a cane chair; a small shelf on the wall. One side of the wall showed stains left by the seepage of grimy water from the rafters that looked as if a picture of the community lamps of Indonesia had been drawn on it. The floor was littered with pill-like rodent droppings. I felt like I had stepped into the production shop of an upcountry doctor.

I could not sleep. Mrs Menon had made me a very good dinner but I could not grab some shut-eye long enough to justify the good meal. I sat up. I checked the books on the shelf one by one thinking I would read something. As I spread open each book in turn, I felt sick. The contents of those books were mostly on *Kamashasthram*. Between these books was inserted another category of books. Study material on birds. I was intrigued by the kinky tastes of the man who had lived in that room. When I looked up, I also saw in the light of the candle a parrot cage hung in a corner—a vacant aviary.

The shelf also held an old album. Initially, I felt awkward opening it. Must be full of pornographic pictures. When I turned the first page, I felt a faint interest. No pictures of nude bodies; just pictures of the faces of beautiful girls. All kinds of women. Burmese, Siamese, Malay, Chinese, a girl from Borneo. Thus, women of varied nationalities stood in array, casting sidelong glances, blushing and smiling. Between those faces, colourful cutouts of manifold stocks of birds were stuck. A Papua girl peeped through the split tail of a bird of paradise. Between the legs of a white peacock, a Siamese beauty smiled. A Dayak woman showed her face covered seductively from the nest of a swan. For a long time I enjoyed looking at this. By then that small candle burned out. Darkness.

I made another effort to fall asleep, but failed. I lay there in the darkness with my eyes open thinking of several things. Gradually my thoughts focused on my host. It had been only four days since I got acquainted with Mr Menon in Jakarta. Even at the first instance I had felt a respect for him for no particular reason. A gentleman who had begun to witness the dusk of his life. On his forehead and in his eyes remain lodged the *granthavarikal* of an old, unknown Malayali *tharavaditham*. He must have been quite handsome in his youth. But now the extent of his baldness stretched from the back of his neck to his forehead like a cemented road over a culvert. The remnants of his curly hair, now grey, stuck to both sides of his head—as if a toothbrush has been thrust behind each ear.

I had assimilated some of Menon's life story from friends in Jakarta, as also from the mouth of Menon himself: A serial story consisting of vast and complex, quirky experiences in foreign lands.

Menon, who had acquired basic knowledge of typewriting and shorthand, had stolen and sold his sister's gold chain and left home 28 years ago—and reached Singapore. For three or four years he worked there in several offices. A European shipping company then sent him to Makassar on Celebes Island. He stayed on in Makassar for 17 years. Sometime during that period he married a woman of mixed origin. Frankly speaking, Menon himself does not know how he married that fat woman who was the mistress of a retired Dutch military officer (Mrs Matilda Menon was a sheep with curly russet hair scattered all over her scalp). It just so happened. Even before the end of the first year of marriage Menon repented his reckless adventure. She was a *thadaka.* She seasoned the simpleton that Menon was with the lashes of the whip that was her tongue. Menon became, completely, the slave of 'Matty'.

Gradually, a change came over his philosophy of life. If life doesn't follow the path chosen, follow life in the path that it takes, with head bowed; the sanctuaries of contentment will not go undiscovered. If one moves forward like a river, it is impossible to back track even an inch—isn't life such a gush of experiences!

Menon would often daydream of returning to his hometown, marrying a nice Malayali girl to begin life anew. That did not come to be. So he decided that he would live on with the wife that he had—and children too, in time to come—and end the drama of life in Makassar itself. Five years passed this way. Matilda did not conceive. Menon realized that she was a *machi.* The desire to become a father seared him continuously.

Menon did not have the courage to discard Matilda. She lay coiled and knotted around him like a python.

One day when Menon went to his office, he learnt that the company had decided to close down their office in Makassar and that all the employees were being terminated with a compensation of three months' wages. He did not inform Matilda; instead he sent her to live with her mother for a few days in a village far away. Menon's plan was to collect the money due to him from the company and board a cargo vessel of the firm and escape to Jakarta. Menon hurriedly completed all the preparations and bade farewell mentally to Makassar, to his past life there and to Matty who had ruled over him for the last five years—and arrived at the *bundar*. Lo and behold! There stood Matilda with boxes and bundles of luggage, fully prepared to travel, waiting for him! As if nothing unusual had transpired, she said to Menon: 'Man, our thermos flask is broken. A flask is imperative for travel on a ship. Be off and get a thermos flask quickly.'

Menon had concluded that when she found out his treachery, Matty would pound him to death in full public view. Matty's behavior consoled him, amazed him. He ran to the market and looked around for a thermos flask.

On the third day of leaving Makassar, the Menons disembarked at Tanjung Priok in Jakarta. And thus, they live on here happily to this day.

I had heard too that they had a daughter, but I did not see the daughter anywhere there. The couple behaved in a very affectionate manner with each other. The change in the conduct of Mrs. Menon must have come about with the arrival of that offspring. Where is that daughter? I also remembered that Menon had said nothing to me about the daughter who had given their life the fragrance of peace.

Thereafter, in an unknown hour of the night, I fell asleep. The next morning Menon came to my room holding a cup of hot tea for me.

'Did you sleep well?' He asked with concern.

I spoke the truth: 'Somehow, I couldn't sleep. Must be because the place is new to me.'

'No. It is because the place is old.' Menon smiled, revealing two gold-capped teeth in his mouth. 'This is a room that has remained locked for six months.'

'Mr Menon, who was the person using this room?' I asked as I sipped my tea.

'Why, did some ghosts visit you?'

'Nothing of the sort happened. But the beauties and birds of Eastern Asia seem to be residing here.' I said, pointing to the album.

'I consider this room as an abandoned temple,' Menon spoke like a philosopher, 'And that album and those books the withered *nirmalyam*.'

'I couldn't understand what you said ...?'

'If you must understand then a lot has to be said.'

'Then speak up—let me hear the tale.'

Menon remained silent for a while. Then, without giving me any indication of what was going to be said, began to relate the story:

'It was 13 years ago. Matty and I had reached the *bundar* to leave Makassar for good and travel to Jakarta. On Matty's request, I had gone to Bajat to buy a thermos flask. When I returned with the flask, I was mildly surprised to see a sprightly little child seated on Matty's lap—but felt sad too in the same instant. Even after five years of marriage we had not been blessed with an offspring.

A Chinese woman was standing there talking to Matty.

When I came near, Matty said: 'Hey, look! This Chinese woman wants to sell this child. Why don't we buy it? It is a very charming kid.'

I looked at that toddler closely. A female child aged around a year and a half. Curly black hair. Large dark eyes. Tender body the assorted colour of rice bran. From her facial features, it could be concluded that she was a child born to an Indian. That little thing kept smiling, looking at my face without averting her eyes.

'How can we believe that this child is this Chinese woman's?' I asked Matty.

'The baby was indeed born to this woman; the point of doubt is only about its father.' Matty said caressing the child's curly locks. Just then that child too lisped something in Chinese.

Matty continued: 'Whatever be, so be it. We will buy the kid and rear it. Anyway we are leaving this place. People will presume it is our own child even without an explanation.'

Matty smiled meaningfully. The same instant, my heart too broke into a smile. The intoxicating dreams of motherhood and fatherhood conjoined. As if in recognition of it, the child too chuckled bashfully.

I looked over that Chinese woman intently. The flushed ripples of youthful freshness and grace played on her cheeks. On the left side of her chin was a black mole, the size of the seed of *kunni* that added a *thilakam* to her beauty. Her dressing was rustic. Studying her skirt and attitude, she did not appear to be in acute poverty. That she did not love the child was obvious. As far as she was concerned, carrying around that dark child was a disgrace—the conspicuous symbol of the sin she committed. Her attitude indicated that she wanted to dispose of that burden howsoever.

We did not have to bargain for long. I gave her 150 guilders. She took the money and stuck it in the pocket of her black silk skirt; then picked up the kid and, kissing it one last time, she handed it to me saying something in Chinese and walked away. That is when I noticed that the girl limped.

That child did not wail to go with her. However, the smile on its face had vanished. As if lost in some philosophical thought, it looked into my eyes with an unusual expression, holding tightly the tie of my dress over my chest. That day, on the ship itself, we gave the child a name: Kalyani. It was my mother's name.

Thus, we reached here in Jakarta. The very next day, I got a temporary job as a storekeeper at the wharf at Tanjung Priok. It continued for six months. Then I remained without a job for several months. Later I was engaged in different jobs—an accountant in a hotel on Gajah Mada Street; a cashier of a Dutch bookshop on Nusantara Street; a caretaker for a Javanese building contractor; an agent for an insurance company. I did not notice the passing of years.

By then my life had taken on a new colour. The reason for that was Kalyani. The only brilliant focal point of the sphere of our lives—Matty's and mine—was Kalyani. Once Kalyani entered our lives an abrupt transformation came over Matty's character and her behavior towards me. Matty's programs that displayed a devilish passion in nagging and pestering me changed to pampering and petting Kalyani. We endured many sacrifices to bring her up like the child of an aristocrat.

It was a year ago that I joined as an accountant in this cloth store of Trilok Singh in Pasar Baru. Trilok Singh vacated a godown in one portion of the building for us to live in. No need to pay rent. Matty did not have to buy a new mattress, either. She would extricate one or two paper-wrapped parcels of silk cloth from the bundles of cloth stacked along the wall on one side of the room and use them as mattresses.

One day I was standing as usual on the small balcony of the building after supper and was looking down at the street below. Kalyani had gone to the movies along with Trilok Singh's daughter.

On the street below a *becha* came to a halt in front of the cloth store. A man in a white suit leapt out of the *becha*—then came the sound of boots pounding up the stairs of the building.

It was a person who had come to reside in the upper floor of the shop. I had gathered that it was Trilok Singh himself who had taken him in. Said that his name is De. Nothing more was known of the man. Not even when I tried to find out. Where does he belong? What is his job? Nothing could even be guessed. Both in his appearance and behavior there was an element of mystery. He was a peculiar person who did not reveal either by his colour or behavior whether he was Eurasian or Javanese or Indian. The matter of his age too was similarly vague. He could be anywhere between twenty-five and forty-five. His name too was puzzling—De was a monosyllable that could suit a Eurasian, or a Javanese or an Indian. That man with a flat small face, a beautiful prominent nose and slightly deep-set dark eyes also had a peculiar gaze and an unusual gait. There seemed to be an unknown magical power in his look. His dressing style was the most modern—who was this man? A CID? An agent for black marketers? Or some eccentric Kuberan who roams the streets in disguise? Whoever he was, even when I saw him for the first time, a belief had got into me that this man was someone whose proximity must be avoided. He would at times stare at Kalyani in a disturbing way: the look of a black magician. My revulsion for him gradually turned to hatred. A couple of times he had come and made as if to talk with me. I did not make any attempt to expel him only because it was my proprietor Trilok Singh who had put him up in a room next to mine.

He walked across the verandah to his room, making a click-clack sound as if an *ottakurukkan* had gone into its den. That man had no companions. He kept a mynah. He had taught that bird all kinds of languages. I could hear him chatting to that bird as if to a friend.

I looked down at the street once more. I couldn't see Kalyani return. The street was very crowded. It was the rush when the show ended. After some time all the noise and bustle subsided. The street became calm like before. The '*krimkrinim*' sound of the bells of *bechas* rang out intermittently.

'*Huh-ong-huy-Man! Man! Man!*'—a devilish scream rent the air! It was from the room. Realizing that it was Matty's voice, I rushed towards the room. Did that black magic fellow startle and attack her?

When I entered the room Matty could not be seen. '*Hoong-hou-houng-man! Man!*' Again came the sound of Matty's lament. She was shouting as she lay on the cot. The cot was covered with bales of cloth. The bundles of cloth stacked high along the wall had collapsed. Matty was howling from under those bundles.

I tried to lift the bundles off the cot. They would not budge. It was only then that I realized the weight of those bundles of cloth which were sent from Holland, stacked, compressed, wrapped and bound.

'*Hoo-ong-man-kaki inisakeet!*' Matty's wail. Her leg was crushed and hurt. I was standing there numbed, eyes protruding and bearing the bundles from Holland.

'*Pangil sobath dakath!*'(Call the friend from the next room). Matty roared.

She said to call the friend from the next room! I pretended not to hear. Heaving the bundle of cloth, I peered with lost focus at the cot. Matty's eye glistened from one corner of a bale like a shard of black glass. Her arms and chest, stomach and thighs were all lying crushed under the bundles of cloth.

'*Pangil sobath dakath!*' Matty roared again.

Friend, I ask you! If all the bundles in the room fell on Matty—if all those bundles caught fire—I would not, still, call that charlatan for rescue, I told myself.

Suddenly I received a blow on my head. I have a faint memory of the remaining bundles of cloth cascading down on the top of my head and shoulders from behind me before I could even turn to look. When I opened my eyes next, what I saw was that man. He was bending over, his deep-set mesmerizing eyes bearing down on my face, trying to effect a smile.

'*Appa kamu sakeet*?' (Do you feel pain?). That was his question; like the chanting of a *manthram.* Searching within myself for an answer, I gaped around the whole room. All those cloth bundles had been stacked along the wall as before. That was his handiwork. The man had the strength of a giant.

I looked for Matty. She was not to be seen there. The cot lay vacant.

Understanding the reason for my silent quest, he said: 'Mrs Menon was not bruised. She has gone to the bathroom to rub down with warm water. You are the one who is hurt.'

He touched me lightly on my bald pate. I felt the tingle of a magic touch. I reached my hand to my head. That is when I realized that there was a wound on my head and that it had been bandaged with cloth.

'The metal strap of the bundle caused the bruise. Doesn't matter. A balm has been applied to it and bandaged.' He said sympathetically and again tried to flash a smile.

I agonized, not knowing how to react to that man at that moment. He was the one who saved my life. Yet, I could not wipe off that old indescribable animosity from my mind. Matty having bathed and changed, came to me, looked at my face and smiled to comfort me.

'I shall swiftly make you some coffee,' said Matty mildly, stroking the cloth tied on my head.

'Let *me* bring something to drink.' Saying this the man went out of the room. He returned in 10 minutes. He was carrying a bottle of brandy in one hand and two glasses in the other. He came and sat on my cot and poured the brandy into one glass and extended it to me.

I was again caught in a fix.

'There is no other medicine as good as this to kill fatigue.' He pressed the glass into my hand.

I looked at Matty's face. When I saw the shadow of a smile there, I became bold. I took that glass of liquor.

He poured a little brandy into the other glass.

'To your quick recovery!'

He raised a toast to me and clinked his class softly on mine and lifted his liquor glass to his lips. Like an automation, the glass in my hand too rose to my lips.

There was a silent pause. The notes of an obscene song of a drunkard on the street wafted into the room. The man pulled out a golden cigarette case from his pocket, snapped it open and offered me one. The distress in talking and the animosity within me had subsided and melancholy had crept into my mind.

I pinched out a cigarette from the cigarette case. He produced a red lighter from his other pocket and, flicking it, lit the cigarette between my lips. I looked at that cigarette lighter then. A lighter made in the shape of a nude dancer. When the dancer's breast is pressed, a flame would leap out from her lips. That trick delighted me immensely. But what I felt like saying was this: 'You pervert! Aren't you ashamed to carry this around?' But I did not say it.

The sound of a car coming to a halt below was heard. In a short while, Kalyani appeared at the door.

He stared at the door, still holding the liquor glass in his hand. Seeing him in the room, Kalyani hesitated. She was peering at him with an unusual expression.

I observed the man's face become pale and his eyes freeze like fish stored in ice. The way he looked at Kalyani infuriated me. 'Get out of here, you indecent dog!' Saying so, I threw the liquor in my glass on his face. Even then he kept staring at her as if in a trance, lost to his surroundings. His despicable expression—that is how I interpreted it—made me mad. The intoxication added to it.

I leapt out of my bed and held him and shook him. My touch seemed to wake him from his trance—he looked at me pathetically.

'Be off with you! Get out!' I caught hold of him and shoved him to the door. Then again from there I pushed him outside. 'If you ever set foot in this room, I'll gouge your eyes out. Beware!'

I fastened the door. Matty came to me and spoke with trepidation: 'What madness did you do? Lòok, Kalyani got frightened and has fainted.'

Cursing myself, I walked over to Kalyani's bed and softly stroked her forehead. My hand felt as if it was singed. She was running a high fever. She lay there like that for three days. The doctor came and examined her and prescribed some medicines. He too opined that she had suffered some sort of shock.

On the fourth day, it became clear that Kalyani's fever was not merely due to shock. Raised hives had appeared on her face and chest. We did not let out the news of the malady. The doctor came and treated her secretly. No good came of it. She died on the fourteenth day. That was the final poison arrow that fate had in store for me.

Four days passed.

That night I was reclining on my mattress and reading the Bhagavat Geetha. Matty was pressing Kalyani's clothes as if nothing unusual had occurred there. I suspected that Matty had been afflicted with insanity. I strained my ears, hearing the commotion of a small crowd on the verandah outside. Immediately came the sound of someone knocking on my door.

'Menon, Menon! *Kamara thuthoopu*!' (Open the door). It was the voice of Trilok Singh.

I opened the door. Standing at the door Trilok Singh stuttered: 'That … that man, De, was involved in a road accident and is lying there in a critical state wounded on the chest. He was taken to the hospital unconscious. When he came to at the hospital the first thing he uttered was that he wanted to come back here. The doctors refused. At that he said he would stab himself to death. So the man has been brought back here. He says that he wants to see Menonbhai. Come soon!'

I went to see the man, still holding the Bhagavat Geetha.

'Mr. Singh, you may leave. Let me talk for a while to Mr Menon,' he said, trying to sit up in bed.

Trilok Singh warned him, 'The wound on your chest … you must not move.' Singh and his companions left, leaving just the two of us in the room.

I glanced at him sympathetically. All the blood had drained from his body and he was pale as paper. The wound on his chest had been bandaged with cloth. He kept looking intensely at my face and would not speak.

'Mr De, my heart truly aches that such a disaster has befallen you,' I said with remorse, recalling my ruthless behavior the other day.

'Mr Menon, don't call me De. Call me Damu.'

I was stunned to hear his reply. He was speaking in chaste Malayalam!

'So are you a Malayali?' I asked him in Malayalam.

'Yes. I was born in the land of Malayalam. But it is over 26 years since I left my place.' He pressed his hand to his chest and shuddered a little. His face revealed that he was suffering acute pain.

'I will not survive. I have only one wish before I die. I want to see Kalyani.'

I remained silent.

He resumed: 'The only reason that I insisted on being brought back here when I regained consciousness at the hospital was just to see her. I knew that if I had sent word to you, you would not have sent her to me. Because you have misunderstood me. I wish to see Kalyani the same way I want to see my little sister before me again. I have loved only two persons sincerely in my life: my sister Kalyani and the girl I loved—no, I won't mention her name. The former died; the latter cheated me. That is where my new life began.'

He gestured for water. I poured the water from the narrow-necked earthen pot into a glass and handed it to him.

'I do not have the time to tell you my life story in elaborate detail. Nor do I have the desire to do so. I will relate some select incidents of my life only in the belief that you will not desist from showing the mercy of bringing Kalyani to me when you have heard my story.

I was the only nephew of a prosperous *tharavad* in an interior part of Malabar. That old *tharavad*—which had on one side a shrine for snake worship and a temple for the goddess on the other, also had a large pond with steps leading down to the water and also a *padipura* and a paddy threshing ground—which must have by now crumbled to the ground, with plants and creepers growing wild around it in likeness of a forest. It is said that it was a cursed *tharavad.* Some *karanavar* became mentally imbalanced and jumped to his death into the pond. My mother died of a snake bite. Only my little sister Kalyani and I remained in the *tharavad*. Kalyani, with her curly dark hair and eyes as black as the Kakkapoo flower, was my very life. I will not describe her too much. Mr Menon, my little sister was the identical twin of your daughter Kalyani; she passed away at the age of fifteen, a victim of small pox.

I would've left my home that day itself, if it were not for that other girl who had stolen my heart. The uncle of that enchantress whom I had loved secretly from a very tender age, was the *amsam adhikari*.

Would you believe it? I had sworn that I would not touch another girl except her in my life. It is doubtful whether any man in the world has ever taken such a vow. I honored my pledge. I was a staunch believer of God. Only a staunch believer will fall into such stupidity. I had a lot of liberty in her house. Our marriage was a matter decided years ago. But not once did I so much as touch her pure form. I preserved that fruit for the nuptial night.

The day of our wedding was fixed. Four days before that day, I saw with my own eyes the final act of that farce: the scene of the caretaker of the *adhikari*—a swarthy fat man who looked like a bear—going into the bedroom of my darling girl and the door closing after him.

From that moment onwards I became a devil. I left home. On the designated night of my wedding, I was in a hotel in Madras. From Madras I reached Burma. From Burma onward to Assam—then to Malaya—to the eastern islands. I despised all the women in the world. I was not satisfied merely with hating them. Take revenge on them: that was the penance I had adopted. Pretend to be in love with virgins, seduce them and cheat them. That has been my occupation for 26 years. Like a clever hunter mimics the cry of birds and lures them only to shoot them down, I produced the fake tone of love to attract young girls and slaughtered their chastity. My complex and mysterious life is a serial tale of the murder of purity. Thus finally, I reached here in Jakarta.

As I was climbing the stairs to move into the room upstairs in this building, there stands on the top step blocking my way, my little sister, Kalyani. I gave a start. I could not believe that sight. Widening her black eyes she looked at me pitiably, '*Kunhetta*, *have you forgotten your sister?'* That was the question pregnant with meaning which was tottering in her look. Suddenly she vanished—into your room.

I went back to my room and sat for a long time, supporting my forehead in my hands. It was an experience as if the malady afflicting the neurotic person is cured instantaneously by a blow received on a vital spot in his body. My sister is not dead; she lives hidden in the world of women. She must have lain hidden in many of the girls I deceived.

'Kalyani!' It sounded to me like the voice of the Formless. It was only later that I realized that it was you calling Kalyani. Fate in its mischief had planned everything—Kalyani!

I yearned to see my sister once more. But Mr Menon, you misunderstood me. Now in the final moment of my life here I am, longing to have a glimpse of her. Please call Kalyani …'

That man squeezed my hand with the ache in his heart. He gazed into my face with tears in his eyes. I too could not contain my tears. Stroking his hand, I said with a cracked voice, looking at the distant sky: 'Damu, she cannot hear our call. She has gone to a place where calls are not heard. Kalyani is no more. The same small pox that stole your sister from you, took away my Kalyani too ...'

He lay there like a ghost gazing into my face. Then a smile slowly spread on his lips.

'Mr Menon, will I live?'

'It is my belief that you will live. May your life blossom and revel in another manner!'

Long silence.

Breaking that silence, I said: 'Damu, now that you have told me all your heart's secrets openly, I do not have the mind to hide any secret from you. I shall say it: Kalyani was not my biological daughter.'

'Huh?'

'I had adopted her. Kalyani was a child I bought from a Chinese woman in Makassar.'

That man shot that ghostly glance at my face again.

'The daughter of a Chinese woman in Makassar?'

He lay back with his eyes closed for a long time. Then suddenly he sat up.

In a suppressed, choked voice he asked me: 'That Chinese woman in Makassar … Mr Menon, tell me; was she lame?'

That question did not surprise me. Noting the resemblance of the features of this man to Kalyani's, I had guessed it.

I said in a calm voice: 'Yes. The Chinese woman in Makassar did have a limp.'

He lay still for a long time. Then sitting up like a healthy man, he spoke in a firm voice: 'I shall not die. I want to live. I will live.'

He did not die. He recovered in a week. One morning he came to my room carrying his bag, all dressed up.

'Mr Menon, let the keys of my room be here. I'll just step out for a while.'

'Where are you going?' I asked with some anxiety.

'I'll come back.'

Saying so much as he walked down the staircase, head bowed, I called out: 'Damu, don't go too far; you haven't recovered fully yet.'

I do not know if he heard me. He did not return that day. Nor the next day. I opened his room and took a look. That bird cage lay vacant. He had gone after setting free that mynah.

He has not come back to this day.'

Spotted Deer

Pulliman

ONE

Kudagu (Coorg)! Dense, beautiful forests with its abundance of trees, cloaked in mist. Contiguous ranges of hills! Precipitous rock formations! Fissures which defy visibility! Valleys that peer into the abyss of the earth! Dales immersed in penance through eons seeking but a glimmer of light! Lakes! The incessant whistling of solitude that causes a numbness to spread in the auditory nerves. Forest streams that seem to run amok, terrified like the recently widowed. Growling brooks and rivulets. Descend some more to expansive pepper gardens, coffee plantations, orange orchards; next enter the plains beyond—mossy green paddy fields, *manakal* thatched with grass, temples dedicated to the god of the mountain, narrow lanes, men with belligerent facial expressions, women who look like wood nymphs. Yes, Coorg is veritably a *Yakshisamrajyam*—a patch of homeland which remains trapped between Mysore in Karnataka and Malabar.

Paddy is harvested there only once annually; the rest of the year is spent in hunting and other pursuits of pleasure by the natives. Wearing just a thong and a coarse woollen jacket, a handkerchief tied around their heads with its loose end hanging behind and with a double-barrel gun leaning against their shoulder, the menfolk scramble fearlessly into the depths of the forest crammed with trees to battle nature and ferocious animals.

The pristine maidens—the most beautiful of all Indian women—dressed in white skirts, wearing the typical Coorgi-style white headdresses embellished with lines of gold—stroll, swinging a cane in their hands, in the vast gardens bathed in the rays of the morning sun.

On the one hand, if what we see in the impassive faces of men is the coarseness of the surface of rock—made so by their incessant fight with the elements, on the other we see in the fair faces of their women, a snowy cool smoothness.

TWO

At a distance of 13 miles from Madikeri (Mercara), to the east of it is situated the village of Sa Graamam. Parvathy is the headmistress of the village school there. She resides in a house on the other side of the hill. A proud mature widow, she has an eight-year-old son whom she dotes on. Parvathy lives in that house with her son and an old maidservant whose name is Akkamma.

It was a day before Puthari. Puthari is an important day for the Coorgis. The day when the bundles of ears of paddy are brought from the fields and winnowed, is festive for them. They feast on the meat gathered from the previous day's hunt and, inebriated with hooch, frolic in great revelry.

Teaching was done in the morning. After an early bath and breakfast Parvathy helped her son with his homework and, picking up a notebook, set out to school. She had to walk to school through a narrow track, a clearing between the lush undergrowth and trees. She walked that path fearlessly because of habitual familiarity.

The whole forest appeared smeared with the golden hue of a beautiful morning. Dewdrops sparkled, dangling from flowers and buds like diminutive joybells. Butterflies of myriad colours fluttered everywhere. Pigeons grunted and cooed; the cuckoo cuckooed, mynahs sang, vines danced in the mild morning breeze.

At the centre of the forest immersed in heavenly beauty, beside the narrow path, is a small lake. With reflections of fruit-bearing trees embossed on its still waters, the lake appears to be an oil painting of a beautiful garden drawn by someone laid out to dry. As if it is a brush used by the unseen painter, a tall palmyra stands a short distance away. Rose plants, thick and intertwined and laden with flowers growing beside the lake; lower surroundings covered with a thick spread of burgeoning light green; a wild chempaka tree with all its leaves shed but flowers sticking to it looking like coral reef; all put together—how exquisite, the portrait of nature! Every day, when she reached that spot, she would experience an inexplicable joy. Often seeing that scene she stood as still as a statue. But this day seemed like an annual celebration of all that beauty. Every flower possessed by the zenith of natural beauty reflected the liveliness of the morning. There was a novelty even at the very tip of every blade of grass. Every grain of sand bore a smile on its face.

She cast her eyes all around. From the foliage of the wild roses flew a quail. A large dragonfly danced, circling over a blooming flower. A tiny sparrow peeked at her from the branch of a tree nearby.

She pondered: 'Alas! Who of the world outside can ever see all this wild beauty? What is the motive behind sketching all this heavenly beauty in such a forsaken, inaccessible, desolate land? What, the secret? Anyone who perchance visits comes with an intention to kill. They use this pond merely to wash their blood-stained hands. This spread of rose plants is to them an impediment. Alas, to enjoy this clarified beauty there is just the void of solitude ...'

Like a worshipper consumed with the passion of devotion, she exclaimed: 'Oh, Goddess of nature, for whom to behold do you stand, so bedecked?'

As if in answer to her query, she felt another question echo within her heart: 'Hark, Parvathy, for whom do *you* come decorated like this?'

Yes, there was no satisfactory answer to that question either. She, a widow—a poor thing whose beauty was mostly on its way out, the wick of youth burnt out before its time—could she even be called a woman on the verge of old age? But what could be the reason for her to dress up so smartly and come embellished with ornaments? She didn't even have a lover from an earlier time.

On that day she wore a Bangalore-style dress instead of her native attire. A green silk saree with large white dots on it was what she wore with a blouse of the same design. She reached out into the shrub of roses to pluck a large one …

Bang!

Her fingers touching that flower, the sound of the gunshot and a whizzing bullet striking the tip of her forefinger, wounding it—all happened in the flash of an instant. She withdrew her hand with a start, looked intently at her hurt finger with trepidation.

A numbness; then a mild pain followed by an acute burning sensation. Blood dripped from the finger onto the bunch of roses below. She shook her hand violently and began to suck on the bleeding finger.

Five minutes passed. And then, a youth carrying a rifle under his arm appeared. When he turned the corner around the rose thickets and set eyes on her, he stopped and stood there wonderstruck, eyes agog.

'My God!' He removed the cigarette from his lips and flicked it away; he came forward, and looking at her from head to toe, asked in Kannada: 'Are you hurt?'

Parvathy said nothing. Seeing the blood dripping from her finger he took a couple of steps forward and, coming very close to her, gripped her right arm. Parvathy shook her arm free disdainfully. A stranger grabbing her arm! A Coorgi woman would never tolerate that.

The youth was nonchalant. He looked at her face with an air of authority. He gripped her arm again, very tightly this time. She had not the strength to break free from a grip like that of an *ayasanigadam*.

He raised her hand and, after wiping the blood from the wound, examined it carefully.

Parvathy's face was drained of every drop of blood; she was trembling inside like a live wire.

'Doesn't matter. Lucky nothing worse happened. My lady, you might have been killed. I shot thinking you were a spotted deer. I chanced to be here because people told me there is a spotted deer which usually comes here to drink water. You were standing here motionless, weren't you? What were you doing?'

Parvathy merely stood there like a puppet and gave no reply. The young man bent over and, picking up the discarded cigarette, pinched out some ash from it and applied it to her finger, pressing ash into wound. He then took out a handkerchief from his pocket and, after bandaging the finger meticulously, released his grip.

She turned speechlessly and began to walk away, but the loose end of her saree hooked onto a rose sprig.

The hand of that youth reached there readily. Though he managed to release the fabric from the thorny catch, his lack of skill caused a linear tear in her saree.

'Sorry—very sorry!' He looked at her face sympathetically. She perked herself up a bit and, pulling a long face, turned and walked away.

She must have walked 15 yards when she returned. Her notebook had fallen somewhere. When she came back to that spot she saw the young man totally engrossed in her teaching notebook. Even when she came to stand near him he paid no attention.

'Will you give me that book, please?' she asked in the Coorgi dialect.

The man looked up. 'Why, you speak, do you—and that too in the Coorgi dialect! I shall give you the book, but let me read it a little.'

'There is nothing to read in there. It is just teaching notes. Please give it back to me!'

'Wow! What handwriting!' Without taking his eyes off the book and ignoring what she said, the youth continued: 'Parvathy mistress! Your handwriting is as pretty as your finger. Mine is as terrible as the talons of a crow's feet. It is because of that handwriting that I have never felt tempted to send a love letter to any damsel. How can I improve my handwriting, Mistress?'

'I don't know. It is getting late. Give me that book!'

'There is a lot for serious study in this book. Oh, there is some poetry too written here! I love to read poems. Mistress, may I keep this book with me for a while?'

Parvathy lost her patience. 'Don't play around with people. Give me back my book!'

The young man drew a cigarette from his pocket, lit it and began to blow smoke leisurely with his eyes half shut.

'Give me my book, will you?' Parvathy moved a little closer to him.

'Why, are you thinking of snatching it from me? I'll give you the book tomorrow—when you go to school tomorrow I shall return it to you right here.'

'Tomorrow is Puthari. The school has a holiday.'

'Oh, yes! Tomorrow is Puthari. So I will return it the day after. And you bring back my handkerchief washed, alright? In case you don't find me, I will tell you my address. Over there, a mile to the east of your school at the Ranger's office, if you ask for the nephew of Ranger Machayyan, anyone will direct you. I am also the clerk there. Name is Devayya … Okay, *goodbye, my spotted deer*!'

He walked away without waiting for Parvathy's reply, cradling his rifle.

As he retreated, she looked at him for a minute attentively for the first time. In white calf-length trousers and rubber shoes, with a red silken vest partially open at the chest, he was fair-skinned, quite well-built and about twenty-five years old. There was a charm in his swagger, carrying that rifle of his. The rippling muscles on his bare calf above his stockings were an appealing sight. His impish expression which implied playfulness, his jauntiness and his fearless demeanour kindled something in her—reviving and refreshing. A jolly fellow indeed, who sees the world as a plaything and life as a *hasyanatakam* …

He vanished from her vision; a delicate residue from his cigarette smoke wafted in the air!

She looked down. At the blood that had oozed and clotted on the ground, she horripilated.

'How sad,' she thought, 'Fate has spilt my own blood on this sacred land! The things that happen unexpectedly! Fiction has no denouement like life itself.'

Engrossed in such and other thoughts, she walked towards her school.

On the morning of the third day, Parvathy set out for school. She had dressed herself more stylishly than usual. She wore the traditional attire of the ladies of Coorg. As she approached that small lake, she felt an irrepressible tremor within. She was certain that the youth would be waiting for her somewhere there.

Parvathy's keen eyes scanned all around. She saw no one. She felt the mild sting of an unjustifiable disappointment intrinsically.

'Stop!'

She stopped, startled, and turned towards the shrubbery from where the command had shot out.

After a while a youth emerged from the shrubs holding a camera. Initially she did not recognize the man. The young man was Devayya himself. He was wearing a blue flannel suit with a red silk tie. He had stuck a red rose in the buttonhole of his jacket.

Parvathy felt shy and frightened at the same time. Above all she felt within the sloshing of a certain joy.

Devayya reared to his full height and, gauging Parvathy from head to toe with his gaze, said with a smile: 'Today the spotted deer has come as the Goddess of the Jungle!'

Feigning annoyance, Parvathy replied: 'Aren't you ashamed to hide behind shrubs and to taunt ladies who pass by?'

Devayya laughed out loud: 'When damsels beautify themselves, dress attractively and walk around, it is the birthright of men to stare. Besides, when the ladies dress up to look attractive and if the men on the way do not enjoy their beauty, it would be a slight—is what I feel. Why do you move about in this desolate forest dressed so well?'

Parvathy's face turned crimson. 'I have not dressed up to attract anyone. It's my sweet will. Why have you come to this forest with your jacket and *kolambi*?'

'That's *my* sweet will. So too, looking at you and enjoying your beauty.'

'Go ahead and enjoy yourself all you want. Couldn't you have brought along a magnifying glass too?'—but please stay quiet; don't deride me. That is the favor I ask of you.'

'Does praise sound like ridicule to you, Mistress?'

Parvathy did not respond. She pulled out his handkerchief from the tuck of her saree and flung it onto his shoulder.

'There is your hanky; thank you. Have you brought my book?'

Devayya lit a cigarette and said, 'I haven't finished reading it. I'm sorry. Has the bruise on your finger healed?'

Parvathy turned and walked away without a word.

The next day as Parvathy walked to school, Devayya was loitering around that rose garden with the rifle tucked under his arm. When he saw her, he said, 'Good morning, Mistress! Are you well? I came here looking for a chance to hunt down a spotted deer; it's a queer creation! Don't see any game coming my way.'

Parvathy walked off, pretending not to have heard what he said. From then on, every day she met Devayya at that very spot. But she never answered his questions. She maintained her dignity and gravitas.

Once, when Devayya snatched a rose stuck in her braid from behind, she lost her temper. She turned around to face him: 'If you are deliberately standing around here to bother me, tell me so. This is not good for you.'

Devayya's face did not have the usual naughty look. He looked at her face—into her eyes—intently but mournfully. A new kind of emotion was creeping into his eyes like a blossom. It seemed as if his eyes were about to spread the wings of that sentiment over Parvathy's own eyes. For a short while Devayya stood still. Then all of a sudden he grabbed Parvathy's hand.

'Parvathy, I love you. I may be an indiscreet person. I cannot express my inner feelings in song like a poet or explain in a roundabout way—I love you intensely. Tell me! (His grip on her hand tightened). Tell me! (He moved closer to her. A soft breeze made the tip of her saree drift and touch him) *Tell me*! Don't you love me too?'

Pavarthy felt weak all over. She had not anticipated this abrupt explosion of passion.

'*I love you.*' What could sound more sweet and sensuous to a woman than that magic chant which issues forth from the mouth of someone whom she adores secretly? *I love you.* Those were the very words that ached to leap out of her own heart. Yet something held back the words which were flailing and fleeing out of her. She knew she was under the spell of an unknown force. She hid it all these days. Not anymore. Still, a hundred obstacles drew a black curtain over her thoughts. Her age, society, circumstances, work, family, propriety, her son ...!

When she regained awareness of her surroundings, she found herself trapped in the embrace of that reckless fellow. In a jiffy she wriggled out of his grasp and dashed away like a bird shot.

FOUR

Parvathy's house is a beautiful small two-storied building, its roof thatched with grass. There is a small verandah on the first floor. When seated on the reclining seat on the verandah facing south, one can see far into the vast expanses of land on all three sides of the house. It is an unforgettable sight: green hillocks budding with natural beauty, bamboo forests interspersed with glades here and there, beaten tracks that snake in all directions.

In the middle of all this, around a bend, can be seen in close proximity Parvathy's favorite little lake and the rose shrubbery. On moonlit nights, she would sit on that verandah and graze on the dreams slithering in that slice of paradise.

Hers is a large compound. On one side is the boundary of a coffee plantation. Next to it is a barren cavernous hillock. At the base of it is a huge rocky boulder that resembles the howdah on an elephant. On the south side is a coy rivulet masked by the labyrinthine growth of cane. The compound is covered with medicinal plants and herbs and 'touch-me-nots' growing wild. But a large portion of the courtyard in front of the house has been cleared and fenced with logs; she has grown a small garden there. A flowering creeper in that garden, strung up to spread over the awning of the *mana*, is resplendent in bloom. To the side of the garden is a fairly large grove of wild banana trees.

It was a bright moonlit night. Parvathy sat on the reclining seat on the verandah and began to ruminate about the events of the morning. Akkamma and Nanjappa were already asleep downstairs.

Her eyes darted towards the lakeshore. That wild chempaka tree that stood guard for the sepulchre of sound looked like a fossilized skeleton in the moonlight. She recalled the indiscreet proposition of that youth beside the lake and the events that followed.

She remembered her childhood. She had many dreams then. The dreams she had dreamt! But circumstances had wasted all of them. Then came her wedding. Her married life was not unhappy. It assumed an ordinary kind of peace and was uneventful. The joy she received as a wife was never wanting. But she had never experienced the pleasure of being a lover. Her husband was a man of ordinary traits. He had his own plantation in Siddhapur and spent most of his days there.

Nanjappa was born, she became a mother ... before long she became a widow too ... since then her life gradually became like that of a nun in a convent ... only her son and her work connected her to the world outside.

And now, lo and behold! The clarion call of Cupid made her ears tingle! A delicate thrill crept into her heart. What could be the source of the new spring spouting in this last stage of her parched life?

Indeed! All vain whims! She let out a sigh. Still she could not forget the attractive face of that young man. His fearlessness, verve, pomp and rigidity of character remained imprinted in her mind as if etched in stone. 'Do I deserve his love? Or am I delving into deep jungle by responding to that trumpet call?'

Her deep sigh coincided with someone touching her shoulder from behind. She turned around. The same young man.

As if nothing unusual had transpired, and as if they were forever acquainted, Devayya said: 'Parvathy! Look, how bright the moonlight is! Wow! Feel like dashing about the forest.'

Parvathy looked him over head to toe. That handsome youth—that little demigod, was he her paramour? Her trepidation shrank. Anxiety departed. She prepared herself to accept that new sacred gift of love. The first fair bloom of the vine of love spread gradually across her lips—she straightened up in her seat.

Devayya held her hand. 'Come, let's go over and sit on that rock below.' He stroked her hair softly.

She rose and followed him. Her heart murmured: '*Are you headed for the core of a jungle?*'

From that day onwards she became a lover.

Devayya was a clever hunter who stalked passion. He was most adept at shooting his arrow directly at the most vulnerable spot of his prey. She surrendered herself to his amorous antics like a little child. Yet she spoke nothing of her own love for him. Nothing came forth from her due to the acute pressure of love in her heart.

He would gather her up like a garland of flowers, and then a coy smile would bloom on her face. She craved to loll like a baby in the cradled arms of her lover.

'*Pulliman*!'

She thrilled to his calling her that special name.

'My *pulliman*! Oh, how I love you!'

Few were the days when he did not chant those words. She never tired of it. An indelible freshness prevailed in that magic spell.

She knew well that she was revelling in a garden where she had no right to be. The fragrance of that love pervaded every thought of hers. Not merely her heart but every drop of blood that coursed through her veins reflected the charming form of her lover.

That he might go away was a frightening thought that she endured—his plays of passion ran like a movie through her mind. She would ruminate on every word he uttered; on the way he stood, his side-long glances, his expression as he approached to kiss her, emotive and aroused; the way he walked head held high, his whistling, the ribald jokes he collected to whisper in her ear, that unexpected tight embrace! The minute she thought of him she felt herself melting like camphor in the wind.

Days passed this way—one month, two months. A year … a year-and-a-half!

FIVE

Parvathy received a letter from her father in Siddhapur. 'I am very sick. I think my end is near. You must come here immediately.'

That very noon Parvathy left for Siddhapur with Nanjappa and Akkamma.

Thimmayya was on his death bed. He wept when he saw his eldest daughter. Her sister Seethamma too stood beside him crying, seeing which Parvathy too burst into tears.

The old man held her hand: 'Dear one, do not cry. I am old. I have no choice but to go. I am worried about Seethamma. I did not have the good fortune to see her settled.' He wiped his tears and continued, choking with sadness: 'I entrust her to you. She is now your responsibility. She is just a child. Very naive. Never say a harsh word to her. Even when I'm no more, I will be with you. I have 5,000 rupees received from the sale of all my property here. Give her 3,000 out of it. I have nothing more to say.'

The old man moaned. They dabbed water on his lips. A little later, he closed his eyes forever.

Seethamma collapsed onto Parvathy like a creeper with its roots severed. The two of them hugged each other and burst out crying inconsolably.

After the *pulayadiyanthiram* Parvathy and Seethamma sold all the remaining property in Siddhapur and left for the village where the former lived.

They let Akkamma go to her own house.

When she walked into her own house holding Seethamma's hand, Parvathy's heart began to throb for no discernible reason.

The next day, Devayya arrived. Parvathy did not tell him about Seethamma. But after a while, Devayya did see the new arrival quite unexpectedly.

'Who is this, Parvathy?'

'My *thanki.*' Parvathy stated in a casual manner.

When Parvathy turned to him, Devayya was staring at Seethamma unblinkingly.

'Look here!' She distracted Devayya. 'She is just a child. If you stare at her she will be frightened.'

Devayya, who was trying to hide his embarrassment and shame, asked, 'Oh, so you are Parvathy's little sister; what is your name?'

'Seethamma.'

That night, Parvathy advised her little sister: 'Never give a chance for any scandal to be heard about you!'

Two days passed. One autumn night, bathed in moonlight, Devayya walked right up to where Parvathy was sitting, on the recliner slab, upstairs. She had decorated herself more than usual. Devayya looked at her closely. It had been many days since he had enjoyed the warmth of her bosom.

'Come. Let's go and sit on the elephant rock. They walked slowly down the staircase and into the moonlight holding hands, moving towards that huge rock.

Devayya scooped her up like a child and seated her on the rock and sat beside her. The moonshine made Parvathy's face glow even brighter. To Devayya she looked like a new goddess.

'My *pulliman* is most beautiful today!'

She smiled, contented. He kissed her passionately on both cheeks. She placed her hand on his shoulder with the innocence of a baby. With wide eyes and in a voice that tried to suppress the lump forming in her throat, she asked: 'Will you always love me so?'

'Why do you even doubt it, darling?' he asked, fiddling with her soft braids and stroking her cheeks. 'I will always love my *pulliman* like this.'

He pressed her close to his chest and kissed her lips repeatedly. Parvathy burst out crying. Though she heard the loud drumbeat of her heart—*that is impossible. It will never happen*—Parvathy was comforted by the words of her lover.

'Why does my *pulliman* plead so?' Devayya asked, shaking her, without understanding anything.

She wiped her tears and sat up. She narrated to Devayya how her father had called her to his deathbed and said what he did and how he had entrusted *thanki* to her.

'You must help me find a husband for my Seethamma from somewhere.'

'Oh, is that it?'

He caressed her tired body over and over again.

SIX

Days sped by. But an unknown disturbance possessed Parvathy's mind, increasing with each passing day. The frequency of Devayya's comings and goings to her house was now more than usual. Parvathy began to watch his behavior with Seethamma covertly and otherwise with a magnifying glass. She could find nothing of substance. Still, a hundred unfocused, vague doubts crawled around in her heart like nocturnal insects. Besides, she feared that her own youth and beauty were decaying and that she was wasting away. Whenever she looked in the mirror her heart beat violently.

Parvathy tried as much as she could to keep Seethamma out of Devayya's sight; just a weakness of mind. One day, when she returned from school, Nanjappa ran up to her and cried: '*Devanna* visited while you were away.'

Parvathy's suspicions flared. She called Seethamma and asked: 'Nanjappa says *Devanna* had come; is it true?'

'Yes, he asked if you had returned; after that he went back right away.'

Parvathy went inside and, without changing her clothes, sat on her bed. She asked herself a hundred times: 'Why did Devayya come when he did? He *knew* I wouldn't be here.'

That night she dressed deliberately. But Devayya did not come. When he did come the next night, she asked him about the incident of the previous day.

'Yes, why do you panic so much? I went rabbit hunting. Coming back this way, I just stepped in to check if you had returned.'

She was satisfied with his answer. She cursed herself for having doubted him. With deep regret, she hugged Devayya, and with a face that begged to be kissed, asked: 'Will you forever love me like this?'

Hearing her childish question, Devayya burst out laughing. 'Am I not my *pulliman*'s very own forever and ever?'

She collapsed onto his chest. She wished she could die lying on that chest. But doubt combined with jealousy began to rear its head again and gnawed at her heart. She began to suspect Seethamma's every action.

Parvathy would come home from school at odd hours. Often she would stay home hidden without going to school, as if she were hoping to catch some act of stealth. Once she smelled the fragrance of jasmine flowers from Seethamma's room. When Parvathy searched the room suspiciously, she found a large jasmine garland in Seethamma's box of clothes. She called Seethamma and asked her how she had got it.

Seethamma hesitated, but when forced she said that Devayya had given it to her that morning. Parvathy's face turned red; the blood in her heart boiled. With the ferocity of Bhadrakali, she gave Seethamma's face a hard slap. Seethamma sat on the bed and began to sob uncontrollably, covering her eyes with her hands.

Parvathy too retired to her own room. For a long time, she lost her power of thought. Then she returned to reality. She sat there thinking for a long time. Tears flowed from her eyes in torrents. '*Never speak a harsh word to her*'—she remembered her father's last words. She reminisced about the time when Seethamma was a little child—how she would carry her around and pet her, and many other things. Oh, what a cruel person was she! Whatever did she do wrong? God, what would be the consequence of all this?

The next day Parvathy went to Veerarajendrapet and bought a new pair of ear drops for her little sister and gave it to her. She had bought many other things too for herself; but she did not show them to Seethamma.

However, the angel of peace did not dwell in that house. It might be said that there lived in that house four women instead of two. Two sisters—one elder, the other younger, and a lover and her rival. The boundless and unmatched beauty of Seethamma and the thrust of her youth were all unbearable to Parvathy.

She sensed for several reasons that Devayya's interest in her had begun to wane. His embraces were no longer strong; his kisses had lost their warmth. *Pulliman*! Had he forgotten that thrill-inducing endearment? '*Oh, how I love you*!'—was a phrase she scarcely heard any more. Seethamma alone was the reason for all this!

Parvathy now considered Seethamma an inevitable catastrophe. An angel of misfortune! The very next moment, the thought that Seethamma was her orphaned sister would dampen her conscience. Thus, as the poet described it:

'To strike with one hand,
Only to caress with the other...'

Parvathy alternately beat and fondled Seethamma in her mind. To wage war with the years that had encroached upon her youth and disheveled it, she brought about some new changes in her attire. The articles she brought from Veerarajendrapet were meant for this.

All this did not escape Devayya's notice. Parvathy was trying to make herself more attractive. Her cheeks smelled of Cuticura powder. Some colour had been dabbed on to those lips. Such was not the case before. That the colour of her hair had become darker than before, also invited suspicion.

What Devayya felt for her was sympathy and a mild derision instead of love or passion. He looked at her without any emotion. But then, so as not to hurt her sentiments, he said: 'I have never seen my *pulliman* so attractive before!'

A smile of gratitude combined with contentment sprouted between those artificially coloured lips. Parvathy jerked her neck and, slanting the corner of her eyes, cast a glance at her lover. There was a mischievous look in the flash of her eyes. The cremains of sincerity were scattered in that smile.

The next day too she waited, dressed like a whore. Devayya did not come. She spent three more nights waiting, perfumed and bedecked. Devayya did not even peep in. On the fifth night he came. She neither showed her disappointment nor said anything. She lost herself in his amorous plays and forgave him silently.

In every visit of Devayya she experienced the joy of finding a new treasure. The fear that her young handsome lover might abandon her and go away, troubled her every moment. She struggled to build artificial dykes of dust to arrest the draining beauty that was pouring from the ruptured dam of her youth. A distorted shadow of disappointment shivered within her heart.

SEVEN

'Kaveri Sankramam' was approaching. It is a time when thousands of pilgrims throng to the source of the river Kaveri, called, 'Thala

Kaveri.' Devayya set out to have a holy dip there along with Parvathy, Seethamma and Nanjappa in a special motor car.

The group returned from the ritual bath in the holy river to a small house which had been arranged for that night's stay. They had brought along with them mattresses and other articles and food. The next morning, as they prepared to leave, it was noticed that Seethamma had dropped the gemstone-studded part of her ear drops somewhere. Though they searched everywhere, they had to leave without it.

Two days later, Parvathy took all the mattresses in the house out onto the courtyard to fluff them out in the sun. When she unrolled one of them she saw Seethamma's trinket glittering on it. For a minute she stood there lost in thought. This was the mattress that Devayya had slept on when they went to Thala Kaveri. How had Seethamma's ornament reached that very mattress?

Everything became clear to her. She recollected the night they spent at Thala Kaveri. Seethamma, Nanjappa and herself had slept in one room while Devayya slept in the next. Parvathy had fallen asleep early due to the fatigue of the journey.

She didn't have the strength to stand in the courtyard. When she reconstructed the scene of that great betrayal in her mind, every pore in her became a pit of blazing fire. She stepped onto the patio. She somehow managed to sit on a chair. Her ears perked. A whistle blew in her brain. She felt that a tinge of red colour had pervaded her surroundings.

'*Akka*, would you like some root?' Seethamma walked up to her with a glass bowl full of roasted edible roots, their skin peeled.

The minute Parvathy set eyes on her sister who had betrayed her trust, she was beside herself with rage and struck at that crystal bowl, shattering it. A shard of glass struck Seethamma's leg, bruising it badly. Blood streamed from the wound. She screamed and fell on the floor. Parvathy merely sat there looking afar indifferently and did nothing. That day the sisters exchanged not a word. Nor was any food cooked in the house.

Night fell. Seethamma had retired early to her room and lain down. Parvathy too went to bed. But she could not sleep. She began to despise herself. 'Oh! Why did I harm Seethamma? She is a young girl. Why do I blame her if she is swayed by the new emotions and feelings which are intrinsic to her youth? My deeds are the products of my own insane selfishness. I have begun to rot because of my uncontrolled jealousy. How long do I have to endure all this?' Her father's last words kept ringing in her mind over and over again. 'No, Father will never forgive me.' She wanted to die. But when thoughts of Devayya returned, the desire for pleasure would crop up again. 'I want to enjoy the very last atom of life's sensual pleasures.'

Thoughts of her little sister bothered her again. 'Oh, what have I done because of my fleeting madness? Seetha is an orphan. How fond she was of me in her childhood! Even now she behaves like a very obedient girl, fearing me yet loving me. But the romance on the other side has messed up everything. All that love and trust has disintegrated.'

Her conscience whispered to her that she must apologize to her younger sister.

She rose from her bed slowly. Seethamma slept in the next room. One had to pass through Parvathy's bedroom to enter that room. It was her practice to bolt the door from outside after Seethamma had gone to bed. She softly opened the door and peered inside. There was a bedside lamp glowing on a table next to the bed. Seethamma was sleeping on her side. There was blood on the piece of cloth bound around her bruised leg. The leg rested on a pillow placed beneath it.

Seeing her little sister's pathetic state, Parvathy's heart throbbed with remorse. Sisterly love burst from her. Memories of Seethamma's childhood rose in her mind. An indefatigable force dragged her onto her sister's bed. She sat delicately on the mattress. She again stared impassively at her sister without blinking, her eyes brimming with kindness.

Poor thing! Sleeps like a child. Why should she hate this girl who had not outgrown her childhood? She was a predatory animal to harm this innocence. Once more, memories of her father on his deathbed brought tears to her eyes. She decided to wake Seethamma and beg forgiveness.

Seethamma moved in her sleep. Her breasts stuck out a little more. Parvathy looked carefully. There was a piece of paper – no, a picture tucked into her blouse. Seethamma was motionless, deep in sleep. Parvathy cautiously pulled out that picture which was peeping out of Seethamma's skimpy blouse and looked at it.

A beautiful photo of Devayya!

Parvathy's eyes took on a tinge of colour. A black pall fell over her heart. Another scene came into view. Seethamma transmuted into a serpent before her eyes. From the burrow of her own heart, another serpent—bearing the venom of jealousy—raised its hood and hissed a few times. You wicked woman! You and I cannot remain in one place. Betrayer! You are not my sister. Beware you me ...

She looked around. On the table lay a knife used to cut cords. She leaned over and picked it up. Like a devotee about to make a sacrificial killing takes a last look with satisfaction at his offering, she looked at Seethamma and, with a hiss, raised the knife to strike.

A powerful hand gripped her raised hand, restraining it. She looked back. Outside the window stood Devayya! He prised apart the bars of the window with his other hand effortlessly and climbed in.

A sound like the chirping of a house lizard emerged from Parvathy's throat ... that was all. Then, losing consciousness, she sank to the floor like a piece of old cloth.

When she came to, she found herself lying on the mattress in her own room. Devayya was standing beside her. She glared up at him; she remained motionless and looked piercingly at him. Devayya asked her several questions. She heard nothing—she did not relinquish that serpentine look. She lay there for half an hour with that look in her eyes. Then she emitted a terrible '*Kee*' sound of a devil. With that she lost her consciousness once more. Hearing this sound Seethamma woke with a start and came limping into the room. Seeing her unconscious sister, she screamed aloud.

'Don't be afraid,' Devayya comforted her. 'It's just typhoid fever.'

EIGHT

Parvathy was bedridden. She began to show symptoms of depression. She spoke not at all. When she saw Devayya she would stare at him with no sense of time. Devayya brought a doctor from Madikeri. The treatment reduced the symptoms of depression very slightly after a month. But her health had splintered like shattered glassware.

She could not rise from bed. She became as scrawny as an earthworm. Her face had paled like a *nandyarvattam* flower and her cheeks had hollowed like the withered rind of an orange. Like little pools of water left in scattered pits in a pond dried by the summer heat, the faint traces of a beauty withered by sickness and age were still lodged in her sunken eyes. She disintegrated to such a pathetic extent that nothing could put her back together again.

Devayya would visit regularly but not to see her. Once in a while he would step into her room. 'How do you feel? Have you had your medicine?' He would repeat the same questions every time.

Once when Devayya came, she raised her head and made as if to say something. Devayya bent over the cot. She looked around suspiciously and asked in a suppressed tone, 'Have you told her about us?'

'No,' Devayya answered with a sympathetic smile.

She pressed his hand. Her eyes filled with tears. 'I am selfish; you must make me a promise as compensation for having loved me.'

'What is it?'

'You must never tell her that.'

Parvathy broke down. Before she collapsed, Devayya supported her and laid her down on the mattress.

Devayya sat down on a chair beside her cot. Parvathy lay back with her eyes closed, exhausted.

He looked at her closely. What a change! She now looked like an old moth-eaten book of love. But there dwelled within her a light that neither age nor sickness—neither disappointment nor sorrow—could ever put out. A self-induced light source like radium. The reminiscences of love which slithered around like nocturnal locusts on the walls of her heart flew recklessly into that light source.

Parvathy could never return to those bygone days. She was a butterfly with its wings charred. All that now remained to feed elixir to her love were the ancient pyres. The only pleasure left now was to gather up those old memories lying scattered.

She suppressed all her desires. But at times—oh! To feel the warmth of Devayya's lips; to press herself against his chest, to stand in his strong embrace. Oh my! A strong longing to re-enact all those love games one by one would often possess her. She would sit up in bed and look out the window. That elephant rock—their own throne of love in those days—would come into view. A sigh would escape her lips.

On a moonlit night, when she looked out of the window she saw two persons sitting on that rock. She realized that they were Devayya and Seethamma. She would place Devayya's photograph before her and play out romantic antics. She would pretend to be the old love-stricken Parvathy and enact scenes.

Once, when Seethamma came into Parvathy's room she saw her sucking greedily on the stub of a cigarette Devayya had discarded. When she saw Seethamma, Parvathy quickly hid the stub. But she could not hide the smoke that filled her mouth. Trying to swallow the smoke, she choked on it and began to cough. Smoke streamed through her nostrils.

'What is it, *Akka*?' Seethamma asked politely.

'Get out!' Parvathy drove her out, scolding her too.

A long while later a scream coming from Parvathy's room rent the air. When Seethamma came running worried, she saw that Parvathy's mattress was on fire. She somehow dragged Parvathy onto the floor, ran out and fetched a pot of water and doused the flames.

Seethamma understood that the fire was caused by the burning cigarette stub hidden under the mattress. She spoke to Devayya that night about that incident. The next morning Devayya brought a packet of cigarettes and placed it in Parvathy's hand.

Parvathy frequently became a spectre. And that love an unbearable burden too. She wasn't prepared to put that weight down even for a moment. She wished to get crushed and to shrink under that oppressive weight and die by it.

At the time of moonrise on peaceful spring evenings she would look out through her window. What all dreams pranced around outside with their wings spread. Abruptly the sound of Devayya's raucous laughter from upstairs would fall on her ears. Why did she crave him so? Everything was over! Shattered! Like a child picking up her broken toys and playing with them again, why did she gather the fragments of her dreams and fondle them? Yet it wasn't that she did not find happiness in infantile games.

Devayya would sometimes come into her room and sit on the edge of her bed. She couldn't bear his look. It no longer held the quality of a lover's glance. It was the look of a doctor visiting his patient. She was not a paramour, but a sick person. That thought made her seethe within—she would then regret lacking the power like Seethadevi to vanish into the depths of an Earth that had split open for her.

Devayya would sit motionless, smoking. She desired intrinsically: 'If only he would touch my burning bosom! If only he would call me *pulliman* once more! Would that he whispered a love-joke in my ear just once, play with my hair again ...!' No, everything was mere fantasy. She was a withered, fallen flower. A battered vehicle. A shattered dream deserving not love but only sympathy.

Devayya and Seethamma would sit upstairs chatting. Parvathy, curious to know what they spoke about, would drag herself out of her bed, move through the corridor and crawl up several steps of the staircase and stand there, listening carefully.

Once when the lovers were conversing so, Parvathy crept upstairs stealthily like a cat.

'Don't kiss me. Your mouth reeks of liquor.'

'Don't be cross, my goddess! It is true that I have had some liquor. A kiss when intoxicated is all the more fun—just one more!'

'This is not a brothel!'

'No. Agreed. It is truly a monastery. This place is Panchavati. This house is an ashram. Darling, you are my Seetha—ha! *My* Seetha, mine alone!'

'But we are not the only people who stay here. Let me go downstairs. *Akka* hasn't had her medicine. Must go and pour it out for her.'

'Yes, we are not the only ones here. There is a Shoorpanakha too—your *akka* is a demon like Shoorpanakha. That demon might have killed you, had I not reached there by the grace of God and stopped her. But there she lies now in a more pathetic state than if her nose and breasts were chopped off. I have not told you about that incident. Now I feel like telling you …'

Chada, Pada …

Sounds from below. Devayya and Seethamma jumped up and rushed downstairs only to see Parvathy pathetically dragging herself using all her life's energy, to get back into her room. They looked at each other anxiously and with trepidation.

'She must've come to overhear our conversation. Vile woman!'

'Oh no, poor thing!' Seethamma checked him. 'Let me go and see if she is alright.'

Seethamma looked in on Parvathy. She was lying still all wrapped up. '*Akka*, *Akka*!' She called out. Parvathy neither moved nor acknowledged her presence or call.

Four days passed.

An uncle named Kariyappa lived in a place called Gonikopal. Parvathy wrote to him, inviting him home. When Kariyappa arrived she said to him: 'Uncle, as I am ill and bedridden my Nanjappa is not getting a proper education. You must take him to Bangalore. I will give you a letter for a friend of mine there to admit him to a boarding school and do whatever is needed. Here, take this money.'

Parvathy gave Kariyappa a hundred rupees. The next day, Kariyappa took Nanjappa along and set out for Bangalore. She called her son to her and studied him from head to toe. Then she hugged him and kissed him on the forehead. 'You must study well and grow up to be a good boy!'

She gave him a rupee and sat watching her son go away, her eyes brimming with tears. When he was out of sight, she slowly sank into her bed sideways and lay there, covering herself completely. Seethamma, standing in the corridor, heard her sob incessantly under her bedclothes.

NINE

Devayya and Seethamma talked secretly about Nanjappa being sent to Bangalore. Parvathy had not talked about it to either of them—particularly to Devayya—till that day; not even hinted at it. Then what could be the reason for such an impulsive decision?

'Didn't I tell you—that she is still not completely cured of her insanity?' Devayya remarked.

'She has more power of understanding and intelligence than us,' Seethamma replied. 'There has been a change in her behaviour in the last two days. She seems very peaceful and self-contained. Those long thoughtful silences and the mutterings have stopped.'

Puthari was four days away. On the day before Puthari, Parvathy said that she wanted to see Devayya. He entered her room and sat on her mattress. With difficulty, she sat up in bed.

'You seem to be rid of all illness now,' said Devayya, 'Drink some soup; it will strengthen you.'

'Hm ...' She looked at Devayya's face with a faint smile.

After remaining silent for a short while, she said, 'Isn't it Puthari tomorrow? I want to have rice with venison.'

'I do not hunt anymore. I shall arrange with someone who does to bring some venison.'

'That won't be necessary. There is a deer that comes regularly to drink water in our lake every night.'

'Who said this?'

'Oh, many people. The children from the school who came to see me yesterday also told me about it. I too thought I saw a deer at a distance when I went there last night. If you sit on the reclining seat of our house on the verandah upstairs, you can sight it and easily shoot it down.'

Devayya looked at Parvathy's face for a long time. She sat there, her eyes focused on a distant void outside the window. Devayya felt that what she said was true—because, even in the days when she unhinged, she had not lied to him.

'Right you are. I will go and fetch my Lui-gun. When does the deer come?'

'A couple of hours after dusk,' said Parvathy without altering her gaze.

Dusk was almost ending. Devayya was squatting on the reclining seat of the *mana* upstairs, watching the lake and waiting for the spotted deer to appear. Next to him sat Seethamma. Each minute was spent with impatience.

'There! Something is moving towards the lake!'

The moonlight dimmed a little. 'It is certainly the spotted deer!' Seethamma said jubilantly.

'You stay still. Let me balance the rifle on your shoulder to take aim.'

The deer, now at the lake, bent down and began to drink water. The moonlight became bright once more. 'It's a fawn. Don't move,'said Devayya aiming his gun, 'Here, one, two ...'

'Oh!'

The shot was fired. He did not miss—the bullet hit the fawn all right; it toppled over and fell. Devayya gleefully pecked Seethamma's cheek. Holding his rifle under his arm and picking up his torch, he hurried down the stairs.

When he reached the bank of the lake, what greeted his eyes was Parvathy's corpse. The shot had hit her. She was that *pulliman*. On the right side of her forehead, was a red spot with a stain of the blood that trickled—like smudged vermilion.

She was wearing the same spotted green saree she had worn two years ago. She held something tightly in her fist. A photo—Devayya's photo. The way she lay there, she looked like a little child asleep with its toy gripped tightly in its hand. A piece of paper could be seen next to her body. Devayya bent over and picked it up. A letter. He spread it open, trembling. In the dimming moonlight, he could not read the letters properly. Flashing his torch light and holding his breath, he began to swallow the lines in that letter, thus:

> My beloved sweetheart! Do you remember two years ago—yes, precisely two years ago—at this very spot you had shed a few drops of blood from my finger? That day I might have died at your hands. But for the space of a finger. I received an extension of two years in my life. That is a major gain. For that alone, I consider myself a lucky person.
>
> If I had died then, it would not have been a death of such happiness and contentment. Now here beside this lake, near this spread of rose plants that bore witness to your sweet nothings, bending to kiss your photograph that you gifted me with, love has taught me to stand awaiting, with unbearable joy and excitement, the humming bullet bearing the message of death. Let the bullet strike

me anywhere—my forehead, my bosom, my heart—but when it hits me, my throbs and throes will only be the horripilation of the sighting of death.

You arrested the languid flow of my life with the dam of your embraces. The recurrences of a thousand kisses, the dancing ripples of a thousand love-soaked smiles—how many dreams lie basking on those abandoned shores!

I ruled like a princess over an empire that I had no claim over, but before long, my crown was knocked off. My throne crumbled on its shattered base, but spreading the wings of love, I grew as boundless as the universe. You did not see it. You saw my splintered throne and the fallen crown and mistook it for the end.

I loved you with the avarice of a deluge. I thought of you with the force of a waterfall. Love may be selfish; still, dear one, isn't life itself selfish? Man himself is the selfish creation of God. But to what avail? My love became a morning star that shines in the departing hours of night. In the sunny glow of novelty, I was naturally forgotten.

I envy none. When youth meets youth, why should old age look back and murmur? I have no complaints. Yet, in conclusion, you must not, perchance, forget *her* at least.

I entrust her to you.

My last gift.

Namaskaram! Namaskaram!

—Your *pulliman.*

Her Keralam

Avalude Keralam

On the western verandah of a bungalow bathed in the rays of the evening sun, situated on a hump in the corner of the large rubber estate, a girl sat lost in thought, staring at the garden which looked like the splintered debris of a fallen rainbow. Ismal the Malay, who was the peon of the office, appeared before her carrying the day's mail: a lot of letters and commercial missives. She jumped up and took charge of it. *Mathrubhoomi Azhchapathippu* lay hidden among that cluster. She tore off the wrapper and spread the weekly open and began to rifle through its pages. First she would look at all the pictures in a hurry; then read all the short stories 'oven-hot'. That was her habit. Among the pictures in the weekly, a map caught her eye.

The map of the new State of Keralam—*new* State of Keralam? What did it mean? Is there a new Keralam and an old Keralam—two of them? Whichever way she thought about it, she could not figure it out. From her earliest days of recall, the Keralam that dwelled in her mind was just one. Was it losing its identity? Along with doubt, fear crept into her thoughts. 'Let *Achan* come home. I will ask him.' Saying so to herself, she looked at that map once more.

A drone was heard from the skies. She looked up. Two aircrafts. Two mechanical birds flying across to drop their 'egg-bombs' over the forests where they suspected the Communist revolutionaries crouched, hidden. It was the voice of devastation that hummed in her ears. She thought of her father, an engineer on the estate. One never knew when the hidden Communists would get their hands on that official who went around formulating plans for the construction of roads and bridges in the forests and hills—direct threats to the hideouts of the Communists in otherwise inaccessible jungles.

She cast her eyes afar into a corner. On the slope of that hill was a military camp. It was the regime of Australian military men over there. A portion of the barbed wire fence of that camp ran through a corner of the estate. On the fence sat two yellow birds assuming silence. '*Manjakkiliye kandal, madhuram thinnan kittum*' (If you spot a yellow bird, you will get sweets to eat)—she recalled reading such a Malayalam proverb in some novel.

That girl child born in the land of Malays hadn't seen Malayalanadu. Still, a day did not pass when she hadn't dreamt of the land of Keralam, situated 2,000 miles away, where hills and mountain ranges, lakes, paddy fields and coconut groves intermingled. Through the characters in novels and short stories she envisioned the actual *Keraleeyar* and their day-to-day lifestyle. The historical stories of Keralam that her father told her had added colour to the pictures she had formed in her imagination. She could never forget the tale about the soldier Parasuraman who reclaimed Keralam from the ocean by hurling his axe into it. That land was a sanctuary of peace and beauty. White army men had not set up camp there; war planes did not circle over the forest zones, patrolling. Yes, Keralam was the land of peace. Oh, if only she could fly to that Malayalanadu!

She remembered what her father had told her: 'When I retire from my estate job, we must go to Keralam. The rest of our lives will be spent there.'

She spent her days eagerly hoping and awaiting that period. Yes, Keralam. Her homeland.

She looked at the *balapankthi* in the weekly with interest. She fondly felicitated the little hands which wrote all those stories, articles and poems in that section. She would like to try to write stories and articles like those in Malayalam. At an early age, her father had trained her to read and write in Malayalam. She used to devour greedily all the Malayalam books that were available to her, not just once but several times. But rarely would Malayalam books reach that remote estate at the foot of those hills in Pahang. The nearest estate hamlets were a 100 or 200 miles away. There were Malayalis on all those estates. She had heard that there was not an estate in Malaysia which Malayalis had not infiltrated. When she went visiting alone or together with families, or when return visits were paid, she would take along the latest Malayalam books as visual offerings. Several of them exchanged books and read them. Even with their outer covers torn, pages faded and charred here and there, the binding threadbare, those Malayalam books always had a charming novelty about them. If a novel or a collection of short stories reached her hands, the next five or six days would be festive. After she read the book twice or thrice over, when she was satisfied, she would read them out to her father. *Achan* was an old timer. *Thullalpattu* and *Aattakathakal* were his favorite literature. She was the one who inculcated in him a passion for novels and short stories. *Achan* had taught her many nomadic songs and brief poems by singing them for her.

'Onnanaam kunnimmel onnadikunninmel
Onnallo mangamaar pala nattu …'

How he loved to hear her sing in tune, this *Onappattu*! She knew by heart the old rustic literary works of Keralam, like

Harinamakeertanam, Sheelavati, Bheemankatha, Seethadukkham etc., and also tribal songs like *Kurathipattu. Achan* had taught her the nuances of the tunes and the typical way these songs were to be sung. Was it right? She did not know. She hoped ardently to hear these songs from the mouth of a native Malayali girl.

Achan and she would speak to each other only in Malayalam. *Achan* insisted on it. She too preferred that. But her shyness did not let her speak Malayalam in front of her Malayali friends.

Moideen *kaka*, who ran a provision store in a corner of the estate, would often tease her in Malayalam. She would reciprocate too. Her shyness diminished only through many years of acquaintance. She clearly remembered the day Moideen first came to that bungalow seeking her father. She had deduced that Moideen was a Malayali as soon as she saw him. That obese *kaka,* in a long shirt and lungi with a handkerchief tied around his head, stood in the courtyard and looked at her from head to toe. Then he stood there awkwardly for some time.

'*Thwan adaruma*?' (Is the master home?), he asked in the Malay language.

'Father isn't home. What do you want?' She was about to ask this in Malayalam. But in her shyness, those Malayalam words dissolved at the tip of her tongue.

'*Thwan sada seeni. Appa maau*?' (The master isn't here. What do you want?')—she responded in Malaya itself.

'I'll come and see him later,' saying which, Moideen once again looked at her from head to toe with a disconcerting expression and walked away.

Another time she saw Moideen was with her father. Moideen stood wonderstruck hearing her speak Malayalam. *Achan* smiled and introduced Moideen.

'*'Nde mole, nnalu ejju nammale oru pattikkalu pattichalle?*' (My dear girl! The other day you made a fool of me, didn't you?) He continued: 'How would I know you can speak Malayalam as fluently as a song bird?'

He spoke pointing a finger at her and rolling his eyes in mock reproach. She burst out laughing.

'I too have a daughter of this age,' she heard Moideen tell her father in his accented tongue, 'She is back home in Keralam. Her name is Amina.'

'Where is Moideen *kaka*'s hometown?' *Achan* enquired.

'At Punnayurkulam.'

Punnayurkulam. The name of that Malayali village attracted her. 'Punnayurkulam,' she repeated in her mind. What a cute name! She visualized in her fantasy a blue pond and large golden lotuses in bloom floating in it. Amina must be standing on the bank of a similar pond with many lotuses tucked in her hair.

How many, many such pretty villages must Keralam have?

She looked at the western slope of the hill. The yellow glow of the sun on those verdant hills was beginning to fade. In the northern corner of the horizon stood tall hills the colour of purple. Again was heard the drone of engines from the skies. The aircrafts were returning after their reconnaissance of the region.

'*Prabhe* ...' Her father called out to her. *Achan* had come. She rose. Holding the page of the weekly with the map in it spread open just as it was, she bounded towards her father.

'*Acha*, what is this new Keralam?' she asked.

Vasudevan hugged her affectionately. 'Prabhe, what did you ask?'

'*Acha*, what is the meaning of this new Kerala state? Here, there is a picture here. It is of the new Kerala state, it seems.'

Vasudevan stood thinking: What must I say in reply? How can I make her understand?

'Prabhe, I will explain. I will tell you when we sit in the garden after supper.'

With that he bought some time to think about it.

Vasudevan took off his necktie and hooked it on a hanger and, taking his clothes off, walked towards the bathroom. While in the bathroom his thoughts were about the question put to him by Prabha. Gradually, those thoughts took on a different form—Prabha had grown. She had crossed nineteen. Still she behaved like a child. He prayed that she forever retain her childishness.

Vasudevan recollected the time when he had bought her from a Chinese man for 10 dollars, 19 years ago. It was the most sorrowful phase of his life. He had received a cable from home: '*Padma died soon after delivery; so did the baby.*' His beloved wife left for her heavenly abode after her first childbirth. He couldn't even see the face of that infant. Was fate so merciless?

Vasudevan was working in an estate in Kwantan then. It was the 15th day after news arrived of Padma's demise. Vasudevan was pacing the courtyard gloomily. His servant Ahmed came to him and said: '*Twan*, there is a Chinese baby for sale—do you want her?'

Vasudevan raised his head to look. There at the gate stood an old Chinese man nervously with a cloth bundle on his back.

Ahmed explained in detail: 'It seems the mother passed away soon after childbirth. There is no news of the father since he left the land. That fellow there is the father of the baby's mother. He wants to get rid of the baby because it is a female child.'

'I want the child.'

Vasudevan went up to the old man and took charge of the child. That Chinese old man was happy to receive whatever he did. Vasudevan gave him 10 dollars as advance. Then he took all the documentation required for legal adoption from him. He gave the old man a substantial amount as gift too. He had not seen that old man since. Must have died.

At the primary phase, the child did not seem likely to survive. He arranged the services of a nurse. He provided the best of treatment and medicines for the child. Prabha lived. Grew up healthy. Vasudevan brought her up like a Malayali girl.

19 years! How time had flown! Vasudevan nursed a belief within himself that the soul of the infant which had died in his native village had come here to be born again for him. He considered Prabha the treasure that fate had bestowed on him…

What is this new Keralam, asks Prabha! Vasudevan smiled to himself. What does she know of Keralam? Still, he thought, mustn't I give her an answer? That is when he understood the difficulty in it. This was a topic that needed to be thought over with a lot of gravity.

'*Aikya Keralam*' was first established with neither advice nor persuasion from anyone by non-resident Malayalis. All these persons had a role in it—Ananthan of Kannur, Abdulla of Kasargod, Sudheendran from Mahe, Pankajaksha Menon of Kollengode, Muhammed Kunji from Tirur, Kunjikannan Nambiar of Kadirur, Verghese of Pala and Kunjappu of Kozhikode. All of them celebrated the annual festival of Onam together in places far away from their homeland, spreading the lustre and flavor of Keralam. They displayed the gallantry of Malayali blood. Back home, '*Aikya Keralam*' was yet to take shape … But how can he explain all this to Prabha? In her fantasies, there is only one Keralam. That sweet fantasy must not be bruised …

After dinner, father and daughter stepped into the garden. Prabha repeated that question: '*Acha*, what is new Keralam?'

Vasudevan thought of something and got up and went inside; he took out an old book from a cupboard and brought it over: 'Prabhe, look! This is a book with its binding in shreds. See these three parts of it? Though they have come apart, they are portions of a single whole book. The book can become whole again only if these three parts come together once more. Similarly, on the first of this November, the Keralam which had disintegrated is going to be bound together and made one again. But two sections of that book have been lost: Gudalur and Kanyakumari.'

Vasudevan looked at Prabha. He wondered if she understood it at all. She was bent over dreaming of her Keralam. May those sweet dreams forever remain intact and fly out to Keralam!

The Den of Bachelors
Avivahitharude Mada

The reason for the six of us coming together like this—whether due to our abundant good fortune or misfortune—has still not been determined. Of all the hordes of people in this world, six *such* individuals—where they came from, why they got together, how long would they stay so—these and similar thoughts had never bothered us till now. We had nothing in common except two things: one, all of us had mouths which could produce Malayalam words; two: all of us were unmarried.

When I say 'unmarried', I imply the extreme meaning of that condition; we were people who neither talked about girls nor thought of them, much less read about them. Nevertheless, we were not women haters either.

Our living quarters, situated on the topmost floor of Kacchrawala Building, was widely known as the bachelors' den. But most had not seen the interior of it. We had not permitted it. Married persons, particularly, had no admission there. Some even called this place, '*Aan Convent,*' meaning 'male convent'.

There was no place for manmade laws in our den. Freedom was our slogan. Though we dressed in a dignified manner in silk suits and felt hats when we went out or to office, inside the *mada* we liked to live like primitives.

That day was Saturday. The oldest among us, Nanu Panickar, came back from office with a small packet tucked under his arm.

Although the rest of us pounced on it, Nanu Panickar, being fairly strong, did not let go and gripped it even more tightly.

'Hold on! I will show it to you after lunch,' said he.

Our cook, Appu Nair served lunch in no time. While Nanu Panickar—without changing his clothes—sat down to lunch and began to eat, waggling his head for no reason, we kept on rushing him. 'Oh, ho! Hurry, hurry up!' We were perched on a gunny with its stock of coal or the gunny full of raw rice. But Nanu Panickar always took a full hour to finish his meal. I will say a little more about this person. He is an accountant, cunning and resourceful. Whenever difficult problems cropped up in our lives, as they frequently did, it is the brainwaves that came to this bloke that have saved us. The things closest to his heart are: playing cards and teaching children. When he loses in a card game, his face is a sight to behold. Even if a telegram arrived announcing the sale of the home of his birth, such an expression of disappointment and loss would not reflect on his face.

Nanu Panickar got up after lunch and walked to the tap, licking his palm like a tiger. He blew his nose. Then he produced the stub of a half-smoked beedi from somewhere. He lit it and sat on a Chambers' Dictionary in one corner of the room. Blew his nose once more (this man had a sinus problem).

After subjecting our patience to a trial by fire, Nanu Panickar unwrapped his package and took out the curio inside.

It was a brass plaque. '*B.B. Babhranath*' was inscribed on it in English. We looked at his face, totally at a loss. A hundred questions: 'What? B.B. Babhranath? —who is he? Where does he belong?

Without a word, Nanu Panickar began to peel off his clothes one by one. At last he sat on a chair like a Jain monk and prepared for a short speech.

'Brother donkeys!' (At the den there was an unwritten rule that we could address each other by any name and converse using words not listed even in the thesaurus!) Mr Babhranath is neither Malayali, Bangla nor Assamese. I swear that such a person does not exist on this planet.'

'Then why on earth have you brought this plaque?' The second member, Mr Y.A. Nambiar—who was lying in bed all wrapped up under the pretext that the onset of a headache was imminent—groaned, raising his head a little. The rest of us did not ask anything. We guessed that Nanu Panickar had had another of his brainwaves.

In the meanwhile a lot of betel concoction had found its way into Nanu Panickar's mouth. After chewing on the concoction, head tilted, he spat the red residual sludge into a trash basket and resumed his speech as if no one had troubled him. 'This plaque is to be mounted on the wall outside our *mada* near the door. And then, nobody will find us out. The contribution seekers of the *Samajam* and the seasoned beggars will not trouble us.'

All of us agreed that it was a brilliant idea. Therefore, the board that proclaimed 'Babhranath' acquired a spot on the outer wall.

Unnuka! Boil raw rice in water, strain and store in a vessel and then make a curry to go with it and mash it all together, scrape it off the plate with the cupped palm and put it down by the fistful—not a day passed without our cursing the fellow who invented that cursed ritual. Nanu Panickar often blamed the Creator to whom it hadn't occurred to make a hole in the stomach through which food could be stuffed in directly. When the ritual of the meal ended, there came another: fluff up the mattress and place a pillow on it; clean the underside of your feet and lower yourself sideways onto the mattress and then stretch your whole body, roll on your back and arch upward and let out a sigh. If it is winter you have to wrap yourself with a blanket too—and invite sleep! What a boring task this is! Catch us straining ourselves to perform all these rites! Till the moment sleep squeezes us and renders us unconscious, we engage in whatever activity comes to mind. Once you are asleep, what difference between a silk mattress and a granite stone? The causative factor of this discovery is member number three, D'Cruz. Not much to be said about D'Cruz! Although he has an opinion about anything under the sun, he has only two obsessions: one, that the suit he stitches must be double-breasted; two, there must be plenty of tamarind stock in the curry he eats. Soon after this discovery, D'Cruz sold off his old mattress to a one-eyed fellow who belonged to a renowned group of collectors of used articles on the streets of Bombay called the '*Jari-puranawalas*', for six-and-a-quarter anas.

Around one o'clock that night, Nanu Panickar had the spark of an idea. He hurriedly woke us all up and said in a grave voice: 'We must play two rounds now.' (Two rounds of cards). Nobody contradicted it.

O.K. Nair slithered forward, rubbing sleep from his eyes. D'Cruz groped under his pillow and retrieved a beedi stub, scratched the patch of leucoderma on his chest and grabbed a cozy corner. Like bees flitting out of a broken hive, Y.A. Nambiar stuck his head out of his ten-and-a-half rupee blanket. Then, unable to resist the temptation of the cards, got up and sat near D'Cruz. Nanu Panickar was already waiting with his *thorth mundu* spread out before him, smoothing the deck of cards. He, O.K. Nair and I sat on one side.

By half past two, Y.A. Nambiar's group was down by two flags. Their obstinacy and vigour escalated. Seeing Y.A. Nambiar's game slipping, D'Cruz lost his temper.

'Why can't you concentrate on your game? Are you getting a headache?' he asked crossly.

Y.A. Nambiar's face changed. Holding the deck of cards in his left hand and pointing at D'Cruz, he said, 'You have been calling my malady "*headache, headache*" sarcastically, often. But you must understand one thing. It is not a headache. "Migraine" is what it is called.'

D'Cruz burst into derisive laughter. 'Migraine? Ha, Ha, Ha! I will never use a big word like migraine for such a small discomfort. Man, all you have is a simple headache!'

'No! Migraine!' roared Nambiar, flinging his cards down. 'Headache is an illness that afflicts commoners. Mine is a migraine. The pain of a thousand headpins dipped in poison piercing the right side of my forehead simultaneously—that is a migraine.'

'No! It is a headache,' D'Cruz did not let up.

'Migraine.'

'Headache.'

'Migraine.'

'Headache.'

'Ass! What do you know?'

'You *chudalamada*! Even if you have hives of pox on your forehead, you will call it a headache.'

The argument between D'Cruz and Nambiar deteriorated into a full-fledged quarrel. Finally, it reached a stage when they were about to come to blows. Nanu Panickar, who was seized with longing and impatience after having blocked a good hand, begged of D'Cruz in great disappointment: 'You just agree with him and give in.'

'Phoo!' Snorting like a wild cat D'Cruz said: 'Hell! Agree with him? Oh, yes? I don't need your recommendation.'

Even after an hour, the argument between the two of them did not come to an end. O.K. Nair was already asleep and snoring, lying on his back like a frog. In the end Nanu Panickar got up and picked up *Higher English Grammar* from the table and went to a corner of the room. He lay on his back, splitting his legs wide like the English letter 'Y' with heels resting high on the wall, and began to study English grammar in dead earnest.

'*Chaya, chaya*!' We woke up to Nanu Panickar's roar. That howl for tea was the alarm to wake us. Howsoever late he fell asleep the previous night, Nanu Panickar woke up exactly at 6 o'clock every morning. The minute he wakes, he must get a hot cup of tea. Appu Nair, ready with it, would be waiting in the kitchen. As soon as he heard the call, he would come running and trickle the tea into Nanu Panickar's mouth. Having gulped all of it lying down with his mouth open, he would snooze for another hour like a python.

Before 9 o'clock, we would set out for our respective offices after meals, dressed in suits and jackets—cursing the man who invented the cumbersome attire—like decent, respectable people. Only Y.A. Nambiar did not have to suffer this daily trauma. This freelance journalist would curl up under his blanket till 10:30.

His passions were three—daytime sleep, *musumbi* juice and Sanskrit poems, and he had one sole problem: a chronic headache. Despite all types of treatments, the recurring ache did not go away. It had been a long time now since an enormous fallacy had got into his skull— that a substance called 'starch' was the root cause of his migraine. Therefore, our friend did not so much as touch anything that contained starch or sugar or was even suspected to contain either. *Musumbi* juice and other fruits or chapatis at times were the only things he ate. He had great sympathy for people suffering from headaches. If anything had to be gained from him, all you had to do was pretend to have a headache. Immediately he would invite you to the Irani restaurant nearby and escort you there. Once there, you could order whatever you like.

In the meanwhile, Nambiar would spread open the file that he carried around with him always. Pasted in there you could see clippings of newspaper articles on headaches and advertisements about cures. There would be a blank space for jottings at the bottom of every page. He would ask you a lot of questions and note down your answers in those blank portions. You would have to answer a thousand questions—name, age, village, how long since the headache began to whether the colour of the dress you wear had any relation to your headache—such relevant and irrelevant queries. You could give any answer that came to mind. Just feign a severe headache.

Recently he had acquired new information—that staying hungry diminishes headaches. This practice was begun after the reading of an Upton Sinclair book on fasting.

That day was Saturday. All of us had found refuge at the *mada* early. But Y.A. Nambiar was nowhere to be seen. Appu Nair is the one who exploded that bomb. All of us were shocked. The news was little else but that Y.A. Nambiar was going to get married!

'That consummate sinner is ruined!' said Nanu Panickar in a mournful voice.

D'Cruz drew a cross and prayed, 'May his soul rest in eternal peace!'

Suddenly, without warning, Y.A. Nambiar walked in. All of us glared at him with contempt, malice and a little apprehension, as if looking at a Nazi spy.

Nambiar picked up his ten-and-a-half-rupee blanket, his headache file, four Aspirin tablets and a metal trunk and climbed onto a stool and spoke thus: 'Comrades! Marriage is an act of revenge against being born without choice; therefore, I am going to get married. *Goodbye*!'

Saying so much, he walked out, hefting the trunk by its handle. Thus, Y.A. Nambiar took up residence in a block on Khan Road.

Back in our *mada* we continued our usual routine. Days passed. One night Nanu Panickar got an inspiration.

'We must call on Y.A. Nambiar and his wife tomorrow.'

Silence prevailed in the den for a while. Each of us looked at each other with an expression of diffidence. To visit a married woman! Climbing the Himalayas would be an easier task. Finally, O.K. Nair came forward. 'Don't worry. I'll set everything right. I have a little experience in conducting myself in the presence of married women.' Saying which, he began to prepare for a demonstration. He placed a stool in the middle of the room, wrapped it with a white cloth and ordered us to imagine it was a married bride. Then he summoned each of us separately and made us sit around and demonstrated how to behave in front of a married lady. Apart from that, he also gave us some important lessons on 'etiquette'.

The next day was Sunday. All of us got ready to visit Mr and Mrs Y.A. Nambiar. No sooner did we set out, than the bad omen of a rotten rain began to fall. By the time we reached the end of our street, it began to pour with a drenching force. We were soaked head to foot. When we reached Y.A. Nambiar's block and rang the doorbell, he himself opened the door. We entered silently.

When he saw all of us together, Nambiar's vitals must have seared a bit. We sat on the cushioned seats placed there. We guessed that cursed female must be in the next room. But no sound of movement was heard from anywhere. We sat there like yogis, holding our breath with our mouths clamped, as if our lips were stuck together with glue. Y.A. Nambiar gazed at each of our faces with trepidation.

We spent exactly half an hour with no one speaking to anyone. Finally Y.A. Nambiar summoned up courage and asked: 'What is the purpose of your visit?'

Nanu Panickar got up and, going very close to him, whispered in his ear: 'To see you and your wife.'

'Thankam isn't here. She has gone to visit B.B.C. Menon,' said Nambiar in feigned distress.

All of us jumped up as if a hail of embers had showered on us. O.K. Nair, brandishing a fist at Nambiar's nose thundered, 'Nambiar, we will never tolerate this injustice!'

'What can I do? Nambiar asked in a helpless tone, 'She left in the morning.'

'Idiot! Couldn't you have said this before? We, in all our lives, have never sat so cautiously still for 10 consecutive minutes—don't you know that? Here we were sitting in meditation for the whole of half an hour. You have to give us an explanation for this,' Nanu Panickar roared.

'Yes! We are all going to yell at the top of our voices together!' D'Cruz issued the final diktat.

'Oh, no! Please, don't do *that*! There are many families residing here,' Nambiar pleaded pathetically.

'They must hear it, too. Let them all come. They must know of the injustice you did to us.'

'Please, do anything but that—I will fall at the feet of each one of you.'

'We sure will yell. Ready?' O.K. Nair gave the command, 'One, two, three ...'

A great cluster bang! A bespectacled woman dangling a folding umbrella in her hand entered the room. There wasn't a moment's delay—with a single giant leap, the leader of the group, Mr O.K. Nair, was out of the house! After him, like chimpanzees, each of us blasted through the door, and stampeded down the stairs thunderously, making a '*chada-pada*' racket, like a landslide.

We started to sprint with not a single glance backward.

In the Name of the Law

Niyamathinte Paeril

The opportunity to see myriad types of people, their variegated styles of dressing, and to study them presents itself on a journey by a '*theevandi*'! The Third Class compartment of such a train is a museum of life itself.

The three of us were on a pleasure trip to Shornur. The compartment, vacant when we boarded, filled up after a few stations.

A youngster next to me, in a blue shirt and smoking a beedi, was seated on the narrow ledge of the window with his back pushed out of it as he crouched to fit into its frame. A fat, half-naked and hairy Nair with an umbrella wrapped in blue paper and some packets of masala powder on his lap was preparing, not elaborately though, to make a concoction of betel leaves, lime and araca nut to chew. Across from me was a one-eyed Mappila with a moustache like the coir fibre of beaten rinds of coconut, engrossed in jotting some calculations on the back of an old newspaper. To his left sat a dark-skinned, obese, middle-aged gentleman wearing a round-necked white shirt and a yellow jacket, reading with great concentration wartime news in the newspaper *Keralam*. To launch an attack on his neck, a large bedbug was advancing north on the right shoulder of his jacket like a battle tank. On his left sat a filthy beast, who clearly had never, since birth, had any association of any kind with a barber's knife, with his eyes closed and digging his nose. A ghastly creature with round copper-coloured sores all over its body was pushing and edging its way forward through the crowd, stretching out its hand to everyone, begging. There was another beggar in the south-east corner of the bogie. But this one did not bother the travellers; he just stood supporting himself on a bamboo stick with his limp right leg drooping like the lowered arm of a railway signal, looking out the window. In a green blazer and shorts, a good-looking boy with curly hair was pointing to the advertisements and notices on the walls of the compartment and reading them out aloud to himself in all seriousness. '*Palani Ponmalakku Hara Haro Hara*!'—the shout that rose from the western side of the coach, turned out to be the belch of piety of the priest in a small group of pilgrims on their way to Palani. On the bench opposite mine was a youngster who was neither standing nor sitting. Judging from the nervousness and uneasy manner of this fellow in badly soiled clothes, it would not be too wrong to assume that he had got into the bogie without a ticket. The place next to him was occupied by an old *Pattar* with a switch of hair shaped like an *elathalam* and a grey beard; he had a large lump on the right side of his forehead. Although he appeared to be licking the newspaper he held open, on closer inspection it became evident that he was holding the paper very close to his nose to be able to read. One foot of the man on the upper berth dangled above the *Pattar*'s *manda*, almost touching it. A man sat next to the *Pattar*, leaning against the wall of the compartment. But his face was covered by *The Hindu* newspaper unfurled in front of it. Apart from all these people in that bogie, there was a satyagrahi, who was returning from the Kannur jail.

The blue-shirted fellow, having finished smoking the stub of the beedi, threw it on the floor and, considering that someone might step on the burning stub and singe his foot, as precaution, put it out with the squirt of a quarter-of-an-ounce of spittle.

When the train stopped at the next station, the *Pattar* got off and four or five people boarded.

All of a sudden, an obnoxious stench pierced my nostrils. Not just mine—the expression of my friends and the other travellers showed that they too shared the experience of that foul smell. I covered my face with a handkerchief and looked at the corner to my right side. A woman stood there holding on to the door of the bogie—she was the source of the odour. On her right shoulder she carried an infant that looked like a wood-frog, and in her left hand she gripped a soiled bundle of cloth.

The man in the jacket, having finished reading the newspaper, took a cigarette from his pocket, lit it and began to let out smoke slowly. My friend took the paper from him and read the headlines one by one. Suddenly, he found an interesting piece of news and began to read aloud for our benefit: 'The local magistrate has awarded a sentence of 15 days to a woman called Pathumma for the crime of prostitution.'

Although this bit of news had little significance amidst all the fantastic news about the raging war, because he read it out aloud, everybody reacted as if it was a terrible news of great consequence.

'Prostitution certainly deserves to be punished severely,' said the man in the jacket, tapping his cigarette packet.

'Morality is the foundation of society. To sustain it, laws must be made more stringent,' my friend said aloud, slapping his thigh.

At this point, the man who had covered his face with *The Hindu* lowered the paper and, placing it on his lap, glared at us. I returned the compliment. Sunken cheeks, a long nose and bright eyes – a small moustache too. He wore a long dress made of a coarse material that looked suspiciously like *khadar*. He was young.

'You talk of morality. Could you please explain to me what morality is?' That man in his long dress asked in a placid tone. Nobody said anything. Either each had entrusted the job of explaining to the next man or, because none had the whiff of an idea what propriety in community living truly is, all maintained a stoic silence.

'How do the prevailing laws help in sustaining social morality?' he asked, continuing in the same tone as before.

More silence. After a while, the gent in the jacket made as if to say something ... but said nothing. My friend coughed, and with a hint of annoyance said to the youth: 'You talk like an enemy of morality. If there weren't laws to check prostitution, have you ever thought how decadent our society might have become?'

'I have, Brother, I have thought deeply about it,' said that youth with no change of expression, 'Your words seem to imply that the human race is not in a decadent state already. You have not given me the explanation for social morality—leave alone, that; tell me how the current jurisprudence is useful in curtailing prostitution. Is the law common to all, is it omnipresent? A wealthy man can have as many keeps as he wants; he can whore with the maidservants as much as he likes—the law against prostitution does not apply there. He, with his wealth, is a demigod who must not be counted as man. Think of the hideous and disgusting antics of some characters during say, around two in the morning on the patios of the numerous shops in Kozhikode. That law is not applicable there either, because they are a breed of animals not considered human, or are eunuchs who do not conform to the rules of morality! Then who on earth are these laws made for? For a small section of the middle class. Pathumma, with no recourse to even a single meal a day, decides to sell herself and propositions someone—the law pounces on her, arrests her and sends her to jail …'

At that stage of the young man's tirade, the gent in the jacket shook his head in uncontrollable wrath: 'So the point of your argument is that the business of prostitution may be conducted publicly on the streets?'

The youth edged forward on his seat. 'My respected friend misunderstood me there. If the government or society can create an alternative profession that is not as mean as whoring, prostitution will end naturally. Even then, if some of them remain, such persons must be sent to the mental asylum. I shall indeed worship a society devoid of prostitutes. But it is when I think of the functioning of the childish rules prevalent now, that I feel sad and angry and, at times, like laughing. The scene I witnessed in Delhi—our national capital—I will never be able to forget. Whores lined the streets shouting, "Babuji, just two anas for a great session (of fornication)." Barely two miles away, the magnificent building of the law-making congregation (Parliament House) stands dignified with its head held high! Brothers, *lajjikkoo*!' (Hang your heads in shame!)

The youth pronounced the last few words with profound emotion. We were all deeply touched by his words. Realization dawned on us that we had heard something that had the power to make us ponder. We remained silent and kept staring intently at that young man's face.

The train stopped at the next station. Giving all of us great relief, that foul-smelling woman got off and walked away. You might say that we breathed fresh air for some time.

The youth was watching that woman closely as she got off the train and walked away. Two minutes passed. The train jerked and began to move.

'I know that woman who troubled you with the bad odour,' the young man said in all gravity.

We gazed at him in astonishment. A woman who had lost all her feminine – even human – qualities; one who has become the repository of a horrendous disease—he knew her!

'There is a history behind her. If you are interested, I will relate it.' The youth said, his eyes darting towards the railway platform.

Though none of us said anything, all of us were eager to hear that story.

With inherent rhetoric, the youth began:

'She, with her husband, had come from southern Malabar. Her husband was a labourer. A smart young man with a steely body. They lived in a makeshift hut they built on the edge of the fields.

He often came to our house for work. I have often been surprised at the way he ate lunch. He could polish off a *ser* of rice in one sitting. Similarly, he would do the work of four men single-handed. He once spoke to me about his marriage. He had picked her from among the *Thalapoli* girls of the temple. He said he lost his bearings seeing her beauty. Just imagine! The sense of beauty of that labourer! After that he began to bring her gifts of new lengths of cloth for blouses, scented soaps and such other things trying to win her over. Initially she did not give in. But by and by, she began to thaw. Eventually, she swore that she wouldn't marry anyone but him. Thus it culminated in a first class 'love marriage'. They lived in their home town for six months after marriage. When poverty and lack of work became unbearable, they moved to this city, attracted to it by the talks they had heard of its opulence and material wealth.

After reaching here, initially they faced some difficulties for a few days. Gradually he began to get work here and there.

The days he received wages were days of celebration for that young couple. Eight months went by like this. One evening he returned to the hut running a temperature ...'

Our train stopped at the next station. The commotion of travellers getting off the train and into it lasted for about three minutes. The one-eyed Mappila rose. He had to get off here. But he had a strong desire to hear the tale to its end. He lingered for another minute. Then, left with no option, he got off, disappointed. A handsome young man wearing a silk *mundu*, shirt and *veshti* took the seat he vacated. The whistle of the steam engine blew, the train jolted and began to trundle again.

The youth resumed the story: 'His fever escalated. At first some quacks and charlatans were brought in to cure him. The little money they had with them evaporated. Her neighbors advised her that it was better to take him to the hospital. With the help of some considerate young men, a palanquin of gunny was made and, lying on it, he was carried to the hospital. But the intensity of the disease or the extremity of the patient's poverty are not certificates to gain entry into hospitals. Recommendation and corruption stand guard at the gates of the hospital. When refugees reach that point, suffering the extreme agony caused by their disease, the authorities of the hospital have a stock phrase ready for them: '*No room*!'

They waited till evening. Then they brought him back the same way he was taken. Brothers! The hospital is not the place for poor patients to die in or survive.'

'What you say is true.' The owner of the new blue paper-wrapped umbrella, who had remained silent engrossed in the story, placed two fingers over his mouth and, shooting out a blob of red spittle into the wind blowing outside the window, said: 'A boy from our side of town had a similar experience. They hauled the young man who was afflicted with typhus fever on a gunny stretcher to a hospital 15 miles away. It was dusk by the time they got there. The patient and the bearers of the stretcher had to spend the night on the road outside the hospital. Even after waiting till the evening of the next day, he was not admitted. When night fell, they lit a *chootu* and carried the patient back home. But on the way, the patient breathed his last.'

'Quite natural,' said the young man, '24 hours without a meal or medicine and out in the open exposed to the elements—no wonder a typhoid patient died so soon.' That youth continued in a firm voice: 'My young labourer too died on the third day.'

'Oh, no! Died, did he?' The blue-shirted fellow blurted out inadvertently, as if he had just heard the news of the demise of his own elder brother.

'Yes, Brother, he died,' the young man said, turning his face towards the blue-shirt fellow, with a sympathetic smile. 'These are times when death is of no consequence ... people die of starvation here and there in our land, what surprise then of people dying of disease? Leave that aside—we will continue with her tale: After she lost her husband, she lived on in that hut for another one or two months. But a city is a place which gives practically no protection to fair skin and bursting youth with no master. That poor thing was determined to live a proper life of honour, defending her chastity even at the peril of starvation. When she could bear the harassment of the delinquents no more she shifted to another part of the city—to a vacant room which was the extension of a roadside shop. Morality in a room by the side of a street! Ha, ha, ha!' The young man laughed out loud. 'Can you imagine sustainable chastity in the room of a shopfront? But that was the fact of the matter. She tried to make ends meet by working as a maid in several houses and by spinning fibre. She tried to lead a life of respect, not succumbing to the surge of passion and not falling prey to the temptations of satyrs. But she knew nothing about the dangerous undercurrents in store for her that would finally subdue her.

Many people called on her at odd hours and went away disappointed. Nasty rumours were spread about her. A woman living alone. She became the subject of suspicious talk and obnoxious speculations.

One night there came a stocky police constable to her place. The investigation that he commenced with ended in supplication with a sheepish romantic grin. She chased him out, cursing.

A week passed. A policeman presented her before a magistrate. Raman Nair took the witness stand. He stated that she had beckoned him at such a place in the night. Then they made a Mammad take the stand. The Mammad stated that he was witness to this woman gesturing to Raman Nair that night. The matter was concluded quite easily. The magistrate looked at her and asked, 'Do you have to say anything?'

She stared blankly. She had much to say, but did not know how to say it. There was an obstruction in her throat. Fear, sorrow and insult crimped her nerves. Numerous eyes in the court room were focused on her. She was thirsty, felt dizzy—she wanted to run, to escape from there. She stood, eyes downcast, gripping the bars of the witness stand.

'*Two weeks in jail; or a fine of 15 rupees*'—the magistrate pronounced the sentence.

You must take note: the Order of Law. She had no one to defend her innocence in court. She, who was barely managing to earn enough to stay alive, had to deposit 15 rupees!? Otherwise it was two weeks in jail—and that too for the crime of prostitution! When she returned after serving her sentence, she would get two names: one, *whore*, the other *ex-convict*.

If she remitted 15 rupees, her name would remain just one, her own.

She stated that she would pay the fine and asked for a week's time for it. The magistrate granted it.

My distinguished brothers! One has to ask that poor soul how many times she had to sell herself to generate those 15 rupees within a week.

The law, to sustain social morality, thereby brought about a complete transformation in her unblemished life. From then on she adopted that very profession. Didn't you see the consequences yourself: a foul-smelling body, a baby, blind and ugly as an imp. Now she can beckon to anyone, the reason being—like I said before—she is now beyond the realm of law as she is branded a eunuch that is not within its jurisdiction. Shameful!'

The train stopped at the next station.

'Yes, in the name of the law, that woman became a slut.' That young man got up, folded and shoved *The Hindu* paper into his bag and said, 'This is where I get off.' Then, turning to the gentleman in the jacket, said: 'My gentleman friend, *that* is the way morality works in our society.'

He opened the door of the coach and stepped on to the platform.

None of us spoke for a while. Then the jacketed gent said in a sarcastic tone steeped in suspicion: 'Looks like the man who just left is a comrade.'

'Whoever be he, there is sense in what he said,' said the old man, shaking his head and preparing for a second round of betel-chewing.

Life
Jeevitham

ONE

The little river flows, skirting the hillock cloaked in green. At the bend of the river is a deep spot with both its banks sagging and dipping with bamboo clusters, winding creepers and huge trees, all of which created a perennial zone of darkness. Occasionally piercing the profound silence of that place, a kingfisher or a song bird would sometimes wing its way in.

At the point where the bank of the river and the descending hill merged, there stood a huge rock. The river, the hillock and the rock—all three were mute witnesses to the events of centuries.

A poor family lived on the slope of the hill, having cleared a large tract of land of its vegetation and built a house there. That place in time came to be called, '*Puthiyaparambu*' (New Compound).

A sulky blind old man, grey, wizened and hunched with age, used to squat on the verandah of that house with a stick for support, basking in the sun, groaning and scratching himself.

Narayani, aged nine, five-year-old Ammu, and Gopalan who was just a year-and-a-half, were his son's children. Their father was a worker on a rubber estate in Wayanad. Less than a year ago he had contracted malaria and died. Their mother, Chirutha, was one of the last remaining members of that family.

She sustained the family by doing a little farming and spinning coir fibre for a living.

It was a *kanakamalyam* of the festive season of Onam. Little boys ran up the hill singing songs of the flowering season with small wicker baskets dangling from their necks.

'Onnam Kunnummalonnadikunnumma ...
... lonnallo mangamar pala nattu
Palaykila vannu, poo vannu, kai vannu
Palaykku pal kodu Parvathiye ...'

Meaningless yet pleasing to the ear, the bunch of *thechi* flowers shook its head. The *aripoo* smiled. The *odichukuthipoo* stood coyly. Little hands started work vigorously and competitively on the dew-drenched creepers and the tiny sprigs of plants. '*Poove, Poli Poove ...*' rang out everywhere.

Simultaneously, a rival group of boys singing another song came up from the other side of the hill. Their leader was a naughty fellow called Kelappan.

Their group reached where the first group stood. Immediately, a small girl pointed to a boy of about ten in a silk shirt from the group and said to Narayani of Puthiyaparambu: 'Look, he is the nephew of Kunnathu *adhikari*!'

Narayani peered at the boy. Two days ago she had gathered from her mother who went to work at the *adhikari* household that such a boy had arrived from the city.

Both the youthful groups began to sing in competition, spiting each other. Soon the songs of the flowering season became rhymes of profanity. Both sides were now aching for a hand-to-hand trial of strength. They decided to commence '*Onathallu*' right then and there.

In order to proclaim war, Kelappan climbed on to the branch of a wild chempaka tree which broke forthwith, dropping Kelappan on the rocks below—all this happened in one swift moment. With that stopped the boisterous yells and shouts of his party, while the local group began their howls and taunts.

As the sun grew warmer, the children began to disperse, carrying their wicker baskets, now full of flowers. Balakrishnan alone remained. As he hunkered down into the narrow lane that led to his house, his leg was pricked by a stinging nettle. He flung away his flower basket and began to cry, rubbing his leg.

'Kathila Pootheelilangkodi vettila
Nalekkoru vatti poo tharumo…
Thumbappoove, poothirule,
Nalekkoru vatti poo tharumo?'

Singing this beautiful song (a typical Onam song entreating plants for their flowers), a small girl carrying her smaller sister straddling her hip came into that narrow lane. She looked at Balakrishnan keenly, and then at his leg. She put her little sister down, ran off and returned with the leaf of *appa*, a medicinal plant, and rubbed it on the stung spot of the leg.

After a while, he asked her, 'What is your name?'

'Narayani.'

'Where do you live?'

'Over there …'

She pointed out to Puthiyaparambu. Then she gathered all the flowers which had fallen out of his basket and put them back in. Thus, at that spot began their friendship.

The next day too they climbed the hill to pluck flowers. They met again at the same spot and spoke. Narayani called him over to her house to play.

The two of them played hopscotch or went to the riverside and built sand castles or played digging pits in the sand. Sometimes, Balakrishnan would go into the woods in search of birds' nests. Narayani would accompany him but only to gather firewood. He called her 'Rani' in jest, and that form of address stuck.

Balakrishnan did not like the wizened old man. He would look at him and say, 'Look, how he mopes like an owl!' He would sprinkle grains of sugar over the old man's lips and enjoy watching the ants bother him.

Balakrishnan gifted Rani pictures; in return, she knitted little garlands of *ilanji* for him.

Once, when she gave him a garland, he was overjoyed and planted a kiss on her cheek.

A little peeved, she pouted, 'Umm … don't you! I will tell on you to your uncle.'

Balakrishnan laughed uproariously. 'What will you tell him?'

'Umm … I will tell him that—'

He kissed her once more. She coyly tapped him once and ran away.

When the Onam vacation ended, Balakrishnan set out for his own house in the city. On his way to town in his horse-drawn cart, he saw Narayani approaching from the opposite direction carrying a load of coconut rinds on her curly-haired head. When she spotted him, her naked bosom shrank a bit. Through the strands of the bundled fibre that hung down to her shoulders, two dark eyes sparkled. She cringed a little and moved on, slowly.

The cart driver whipped the horse for speed. Narayani walked some distance and turned back. All she could see was a flash of blue— Balakrishnan's jacket— as the cart rounded a bend.

TWO

Six years went by.

Balakrishnan was now in college. He had come home to his relatives' house to spend 15 days. He went over to Puthiyaparambu to check. He found neither the old man nor Narayani there. The old man had died; Narayani had been married off.

He went on a hunt the next day with two of his friends. By noon they reached the slope of a hill some six miles away, exhausted. There were no houses in the vicinity. Far across the fields they saw a little hut and walked over to it.

On the verandah, an infant lay sleeping on a cadjan mat. There was no one in sight.

Balakrishnan called out, 'Aei … Aei!'

From inside the house came a half-naked pregnant woman.

'Can you give us some water?' Balakrishnan asked with relief.

She looked at Balakrishnan intently—then withdrew inside.

She came out again with a reed mat. She had now covered her breasts with a coarse towel, soiled and frayed.

'Please sit down.' She invited Balakrishnan to rest, with a smile. Again she stepped back inside.

Balakrishnan felt he had seen that face before. Suddenly it came to him—*Rani*!

'Who is it? Isn't it Ra—Narayani? Please come out!'

Ashamed and nervous about her disheveled state, she stood partially hidden by the frame of the door.

A man with a headload of tapioca roots and fish slung on a string dangling from his hand came into the courtyard of the hut. He stared at the people seated on the verandah and went inside. After five minutes he came back on to the verandah and stood before Balakrishnan, covering his mouth with a cupped hand in a show of respect. He said, 'I recognized you only when Narayani told me.'

'You are Narayani's husband, aren't you?'

'Yes. She has told me all about her earlier days; how she survived then on the gruel she was fed at the house of the *adhikari*—and other matters.

'What is your name?' Balakrishnan asked him.

'Raman.'

Balakrishnan looked at Raman carefully. He was a strong and healthy man of about thirty-five who wasn't bad looking.

'We are thirsty. Would be nice if you could give us some water.'

Raman ran to the next compound. In 10 minutes he was back with a bunch of tender coconuts.

After quenching their thirst they prepared to leave.

Raman asked: 'Do you have any objection to eating in this house?'

Balakrishnan and his friends looked at each other. They were all quite hungry. Finally, Balakrishnan said, 'We have a few birds that we shot on our hunting trip. If you can cook them for us we are willing to wait.'

'So happy!'

Till dusk that day, they spent their time eating, drinking and enjoying themselves. They realized that Raman was a fellow with a delightful sense of humor. When they departed, bidding farewell, Balakrishnan placed a rupee on the baby. Till Balakrishnan vanished from sight, a pair of wide-open eyes followed him through a slit in the kitchen wall.

THREE

Another six years passed.

Balakrishnan became Dr Balakrishnan.

On the day of the '*Shashti Poorthy*' of the *adhikari*, he went to Kunnathu House. That evening he walked to the river bank. He accidentally fell into a large pit on the bank. Laughing aloud, a naughty little boy emerged from the thicket of creepers nearby and came to stand before him at which a woman from Puthiyaparambu came running, brandishing a long stick to beat him.

The woman was Narayani. When Dr Balakrishnan went up to Puthiyaparambu, Narayani burst into tears. She was a widow. Two years ago, Raman had fallen from a coconut tree to his death.

She said, whimpering and sobbing: 'This is my fate. Last year my mother died too. Now I only have this child and a brother to shelter me.' Kumaran, Narayani's child had put on Dr Balakrishnan's slippers and was flip-flopping around the courtyard guffawing.

Narayani said to him: 'Hey, you! Don't you know him? He is the one who gave you a rupee in the days when you were a flailing infant lying on your back.'

The memory of that day brought tears to her eyes. So joyous had been her life with Raman.

'Your husband Raman was a good man,' Dr Balakrishnan said sympathetically.

Narayani wiped her tears with the corner of the cloth over her bosom. 'Then I was with child—Madhavi.'

'Where is she?'

'She is very shy. Hiding inside.'

'Where is your brother?'

'He is a reckless fellow. Must have gone somewhere to play marbles or pick a fight with someone.'

The doctor pressed two rupees into Kumaran's hand. The little fellow promptly put the coins in his mouth and began to roll around on the ground, like a madcap. A beauty of about seventeen, supporting a pot of water on her hip, walked in with her head bowed and shyly passed them into the kitchen.

Balakrishnan enquired of Narayani, 'Who is that?'

'Don't you know? It is Ammu, my younger sister.'

'Ammu?'

What a transformation! That dirty little kid he had seen perched on Narayani's hip 12 years ago!

Never had he seen such a pretty girl before.

The next day, Dr Balakrishnan sought and found Ammu alone on the river bank. They talked to each other for a short while. Then Ammu said, 'Let me go. If my elder sister sees …'

'Tell your elder sister to get lost. Tonight will be brightly moonlit. Will you come?'

'What for?'

Balakrishnan smirked.

Narayani had seen the two of them talking from afar. She scolded Ammu a lot, later.

'What are you up to—playing coy and coquettish in front of men … it is your conceit! I'll break your legs, watch out!'

Ammu cried, very scared of Narayani.

The doctor overheard Narayani scolding Ammu. He smiled to himself and thought: 'Poor thing! The disappointment and jealousy of good old Rani!'

That night he sat on the sandy bank of the river in the moonlight, waiting for Ammu. He knew that she would somehow manage to come. At last, when it was late night, Ammu came by another route and stood behind him. 'Why did you ask me to come?' she asked, choking. Her face had turned pale; she was trembling all over.

He held her hand. With the other hand he raised her face and tried to kiss her.

She knocked away his hand and stepped back. 'Hey, don't do that—I am going.' She looked all around in fright.

Balakrishan approached her again. She turned around and ran away. Disappointed, he waited there for a very long time but she did not come back. The very next day he left for the city.

The next year Dr Balakrishnan came to Kunnathu House.

It was Onam season again. Children were singing the songs of the season and screaming with excitement on the hill top. But no festivity was seen in Puthiyaparambu. There was no decoration of flowers in the courtyard. What received Balakrishnan when he reached there was the loud sob of Narayani! Six months had not passed as of that day since Ammu and Kumaran left for their heavenly abode on consecutive days. The disease that claimed their lives was the typhus fever which prevailed in the neighborhood.

Several years passed. Dr Balakrishnan got married.

In Puthiyaparambu lived a mother and daughter and a rowdy youngster who always pestered and exploited them—living a life of grief and penury.

FOUR

Dr Balakrishan arrived with his wife at Kunnathu House to spend a few days there.

There was a commotion in Puthiyaparambu. Narayani was crying, beating her breast. Gopalan had tied Madhavi to a coconut tree. He approached her with a demonic grin, holding a heated trident-like tool, a branding iron.

'Help! Uncle, please don't kill me!' Even as Madhavi yelled, squirming and wriggling to get free, Gopalan pressed that hot iron on her palm.

'Ayyo!!' A scream and she fainted. Her neck dropped; her face sagged.

Someone grabbed Gopalan by the neck from behind. Though he couldn't turn around, he found the hand that held him and pressed that hot iron on it with total abandon. With a flailing of the arm, that grip let go. When Gopalan turned, he saw Dr Balakrishnan behind him.

Recoiling with pain, Balakrishnan sat down on the ground. Immediately Narayani came running and poured araca juice on the singed spot. The vivid image of her salving his bruise so long ago when stung by the nettle plant, crossed Balakrishnan's mind.

He turned to Gopalan and said: 'You brute! She, your niece ... There is no use punishing you for scorching me. You are an animal.'

'All this was because the gruel was not ready when he came,' said Narayani.

Gopalan fell at Balakrishnan's feet. 'Master! You must save me!'

A black blister formed at the singed spot on Dr Balakrishnan's hand, shaped like the tines of a trident. On Madhavi's palm too, the same artwork appeared, only more horrendously.

Before long, Narayani's hut—never re-thatched, decaying, crumbling and leaky—finally, like a fallen elephant, collapsed. Poverty, like an incurable malady, clung to that place.

It had been two years since Gopalan left the village. There was no news of him.

It was a dark day in the month of Karkidakam. Gusts of wind blew intermittently. At Puthiyaparambu, in the only room that was left of the crumbled hut, dark and dank, sat a young girl beside the corpse of an old woman, sobbing. There was no one to sympathize with her; the whistling wind blowing outside hummed solitary condolence in response to her wails.

FIVE

The wheel of fortune spun as it must. Progress and modernization duly performed their duty. Dr Balakrishnan was due to retire from the post of Chief Doctor at the government hospital. He was a childless widower. Although he had amassed much wealth, there was no heir to enjoy it.

An urgent case had come up in the obstetrics ward. A pregnant woman had been laid on the mattress after surgery. Right away, Dr Balakrishnan reached there.

The mother was no more; the baby survived.

Not convinced, the doctor reached out to feel the woman's pulse. The next instant, he was stunned to see, on the palm of the dead woman, a black mark in the shape of a trident. Dr Balakrishnan kept looking at the face of that woman for a long time. Then he checked the chart on the bedstead.

'Madhavi,' he muttered, not very softly. He turned to the nurses and asked, 'No guardian?'

'Didn't see anyone yet. It is a pregnancy out of wedlock.'

The doctor adopted that baby. He named her Rani. The very next year he retired from government service with a pension. He decided to buy a lot of land in that remote village, and spend the rest of his life there.

SIX

Another eight years passed.

Onam season. In a room in Kunnathu House lay an old man. His body was thin, bones bent, skin parched and wrinkled. His head had greyed like white paper; drooping half-shut unseeing eyes, cheeks hollowed over toothless gums—old age had not made any changes to that prominent nose of Dr Balakrishnan.

Hearing the door of the room creak open, the old man opened his eyes.

'Is that Rani?' he asked.

A very beautiful girl of nine walked into the room, a wicker basket around her neck.

She walked up to the old man's bed. 'Papa, may I go with Padmanabhan to the hill to pluck flowers?'

That old man grinned, showing all his gums. Then struggled to sit up; he hugged the girl and kissed her head and asked, 'Rani, do you know the flower song?'

'Hmm, I do; Kalyani taught me.'

'Sing it just once, let Papa hear it.'

She hesitated a little at first. Then in a sweet voice she began to sing:

'Kathila Pootheelilangkodi vettila
Nalekkoru vatti poo tharumo…
Thumbappoove, poothirule,
Nalekkoru vatti poo tharumo?'

The very song that Narayani sang so many years ago near the rocky ledge beside Puthiyaparambu. The same song! The same form!

Rani wriggled free from the embrace of the old man and ran out joyfully, thrilled with her freedom. Her friends were waiting for her on the slope of the hillock. Together they climbed the hill, singing.

Balakrishnan looked out through the window. He could not see anything clearly. Yet, he thought to himself: 'Oh, world! Are you about to enact this all over again? On the other hand, I wonder how many times you have repeated all this before me …!'

That hillock, the river and those rocks in the middle still stand. The rocky ledge and that thatched shack which were near them are no longer there. Instead, the place is covered with fruit-bearing cashew-nut trees.

Near the rocks, half hidden by the undergrowth and creepers loomed a tombstone. Engraved on it:

Dr Balakrishnan
Birth: 1849
Died: 1930
Death: Eternal sleep
Life: A dream in that sleep—of vain desires.

Love Letter
Premalekhanam

ONE

The first bell rang in the school. The boys and girls of the School Final class sat in silence, awaiting the arrival of their teacher. Suddenly, somewhere in the class, the croak of a frog was heard—of one trapped in the mouth of a snake.

'*Aiyyo*! Snake! Snake!' shouted the boys and jumped on to their benches; the girls followed suit in sheer fright. No sooner did the teacher enter the room than a live frog leapt from Sudhakaran's jacket and fell in front of him. Following that incident the headmaster of the school fined Sudhakaran a rupee. Sudhakaran in turn, collected two rupees from his friends for winning a bet to make the grumpy Sarojam stand up on the bench.

Sarojam was the daughter of a retired sub-judge. All the boys and girls in the class dreaded her equally. She was considered that cruel, morose and indifferent. She had a nickname among the boys: *Katturumbu,* a dangerous variety of black ant.

Sudhakaran was the apple of the eye of the class, sprightly and energetic. He was the captain of the school's football team, a good athlete and an expert weightlifter. Besides all this he was a good actor too. His perfectly sculpted tall body, thick curly hair and large coal-black eyes made him very attractive. He had no particular interest in studies. But his native shrewdness took him up to the tenth standard. His life's ambition was to become a strong and versatile actor like Douglas Fairbanks.

Another dream of his was his love for Sarojam. He loved her secretly with undying passion. More than her beauty, he was attracted to her casual manner and serious air. Even though that love was irrepressible, he lacked the courage to tell Sarojam about it. He understood well her nature and social status.

After deep thought and deliberation, he prepared for the '*samaram*' of confrontation. He spent two or three days contemplating, racking his brain and writing a letter of love; he scored off lines, over-wrote, rewrote it several times, wrote afresh—till it was good and ready. It was a beautiful compilation of love, desire, philosophy and dreams. On his way back from school, he approached Sarojam on a lonely stretch of the road. The minute he stood before her, all his courage evaporated. He forgot every word of what he wanted to say. He stood awkwardly like an actor who had forgotten his lines. At last, summoning all the courage he had, he proffered the love letter to her and managed to blurt: 'Sarojam, I ... you ... here ...!'

Sarojam's face turned crimson.

'What is this?'

'A true copy of my heart,' he said, with his heart pounding in his chest.

She replied rudely with a slight expression of contempt: 'What is it for? To wipe my slippers with?'

Sudhakaran blanched. He said, suppressing his disappointment: '...............'

Sarojam jerked her head and said in a gruff voice: 'Get lost, instead of standing here talking nonsense!'

'Sarojam, you must read this letter, if only to understand how much I suffer for want of your love.'

Sarojam took the letter from him, flung it on the ground and trampled it underfoot, saying: 'Now, be off with you!'

'Sarojam, how cruel can you be?'

'Stop frolicking with me and go away!'

'I still love you, Sarojam!'

'Didn't I tell you to stop blocking my way and get lost?'

'Else—?'

Sarojam bent down to pick up her footwear.

Sudhakaran turned and walked away; Sarojam went her way.

When Sudhakaran returned to that spot later, he did not find his letter there. He smiled to himself, meaningfully.

Two days passed.

The peon of the school came to tell Sudhakaran that he was wanted by the headmaster. When he went there, he found Sarojam standing next to the headmaster like blazing fire. The headmaster was not merely Narasimhan in name but in deed too.

He called Sudhakaran to his table and, pointing to a letter asked, 'Who wrote this?'

Sudhakaran's face paled on seeing the letter.

'Tell me!' roared the man-lion.

Sudhakaran gave Sarojam a terrible look.

He felt faint. It was as if hot water was filling his veins. His eyes went blank. They brimmed with tears. He bowed his head and said in a pathetic voice: 'Sir, it was I who wrote that letter.'

'Who was it to?

'I haven't sent it to anyone.'

'Then how did Sarojam receive this letter yesterday by mail?'

He again looked at Sarojam with eyes overflowing with emotion. She returned his look contemptuously.

Narasimhan asked once more in a firm voice: 'That means this letter that goes, "Dear Sarojam …" was indeed written by you?'

'I have no reason to deny it.'

'And therefore, I have no reason not to dismiss you, either. You can pack your books and leave.'

Sudhakaran did not beg for mercy. He simply walked out, drawing on the mental strength that always stood by him whenever disaster struck. When he reached the door, he turned and looked at Sarojam once more. She was looking at him too. But this time there was no disgust or derision in her look. It was an anguished gaze suffused with empathy.

Sudhakaran came home directly. Then he had his lunch and, stealing some of his sister's jewellery, walked straight to the railway station.

TWO

Many years passed. There was no news of Sudhakaran. Sarojam had passed her BA and was spending her days peacefully immersed in reading. In those days, a proposal for marriage came for Sarojam. The groom-to-be was Ramachandran, BA, the son of Police Inspector Karunakaran. Karunakaran was her father's old friend and a neighbour. Sarojam had known Ramachandran from her days in school.

Ramachandran used to come to her house and speak with her quite freely. One evening soon after their wedding was finalized, while they were sitting together talking, Ramachandran asked her: 'Sarojam, do you remember, when we were in our School Final class there was an incident of a love letter?'

Recollecting a painful memory, she replied softly: 'Yes.'

'Absolute brute! Him trying to give you that letter, you berating him and stooping to pick up your slippers to thrash him—I was watching all that hiding behind the shrubs nearby. The absurdities he wrote in that letter!'

A little suspiciously Sarojam interrupted him and asked: 'How did *you* see that letter?'

Ramachandran cringed at bit. 'I haven't seen it. But—'

'Don't lie. So you were the one who picked it up from the road and mailed it to my address. Isn't that so?'

Initially Ramchandran kept trying to evade the question. Then he said: 'Sarojam, it was I who did it. When the wind blew the letter towards me, I picked it up. I did it to punish Sudhakaran for his mean deed.'

Sarojam's face glowed like live coal. She looked intensely at Ramachandran's face, got up and walked inside. She returned with an old footwear in her hand and said: 'Get out of this place this very instant. If ever you step into this house—you have seen this slipper before; it is the very slipper that I stooped to pick up that day. You ruined that young man's life, you mean beast! Get lost!'

Ramachandran stood transfixed like a tree struck by lightning.

'Get out!' she roared.

The roar of that little lioness brought him to his senses. Without a word, with no courage to even look back, he walked out.

The very next day, Sarojam set out for Bombay where her uncle worked, for she thought a change of place would give her peace of mind. Accompanying her on her journey was her younger uncle and a servant.

The time was five in the morning. The train was a mere quarter of an hour from Pune. She suddenly realized that her box of jewellery had disappeared. She had no inkling of when it was robbed. She got off the train at Pune and apprised the stationmaster of the theft. He in turn promptly informed the police.

As she had no time to linger in Pune, she continued her journey to Bombay where her uncle Madhavan met the train at Victoria Terminus.

Sarojam, who was very upset, informed her uncle of the theft. Madhavan forthwith contacted the Bombay Police and sought their help.

Madhavan and his family were staying in a large building in Girgaum. Sarojam, though she had heavenly comforts and freedom there, remained depressed about the loss of her jewellery box. That casket contained gems and ornaments valued at around 50,000 rupees. But gradually she could not stay away from the luxury and flamboyance of that magic city. She participated in the hundreds of amusements and thousands of visual joys of the place.

The next day an old Muslim knocked on their door, carrying a large bag.

A servant opened the door. The visitor gave him a card and said, 'I would like to meet Miss Sarojam.'

'Ahmed Shafi – Bombay CID' was printed on that card.

'Ask him to come in,' said Sarojam to the servant.

Smiling, Ahmed Shafi came into the room and, saluting Sarojam, he sat on a chair offered by Sarojam and watched her keenly through his blue-tinted glasses. Her face did not have the flush of earlier days now. A couple of pimples on her left cheek only served to make her more beautiful. She was in a blue saree with a border embroidered in white—a Parsee tradition.

Shafi began the conversation: 'Madam, wasn't it your jewellery box that was stolen somewhere near Pune?'

'Yes, yes! Why, has it been traced?' Sarojam asked anxiously.

Shafi opened his bag and took out the jewellery casket.

'Please check if all your ornaments are in there.'

When she saw the jewellery casket, Sarojam was beside herself with happiness. She had given up all hopes of getting it back. She began to take out the ornaments one at a time and checking it before placing it on the table. Then she opened a tiny gold case. Suddenly, the glow on her face vanished and she became pale. Her delighted face turned ashen and reflected disappointment.

'Madam, I hope nothing has fallen out of it,' said Shafi, who was observing her closely.

'Something that was in this case is missing,' she said, her voice breaking.

'What was it?' He wrinkled his brow.

Without answering him, Sarojam started to search inside the jewel box again.

'All the ornaments are here. Can't understand how that thing alone which was in the gold case is missing.'

'Madam, tell me what was in it? Was it a precious stone?'

'Something more precious,' said Sarojam, still staring into that gold case.

He moved a little closer to Sarojam and pleaded: 'Madam, please tell me without hiding anything. We are here to help the people of society. A dying man must not hide anything from a Christian priest; similarly a client must not hold back anything from his lawyer; so too, a complainant must not suppress anything from the policeman. We will retrieve the lost article somehow. Tell me, what was it?'

Almost to herself she said, 'It was a letter.'

'Oh, is that all?' Shafi stroked his grey beard and prepared to leave.

She began to juggle with a gold chain and said in a shy tone mixed with the pain of recollection, 'It was a love letter.'

Shafi again spoke with empathy and anxiety: 'So you have a love story also to tell.'

Sarojam fell silent.

'Madam, please tell all. Old as I am now, I too am a victim of unrequited love. I have plenty of worldly experience too. Besides, I know psychology. If I can help you in any way, I would consider it a personal gain.'

She said nothing.

'Some secrets have entered your life, isn't it, Madam?'

'Not *secrets*. Just one, a secret of love,' she said morosely. The gravity on her face she wore seven years ago had again crept up there.

She continued: 'I do not mind talking about that love story. I was then a School Final student. I began to like a classmate of mine, but I was a very ill-tempered girl who was conceited and obstinate too. If that young fellow had sensed my feelings for him, it would be damaging to my solemnity—so I thought then. So when my heartthrob, that young man—Sudhakaran was his name—approached me with a love letter, I felt my dignity had been bruised. I don't know the philosophy or psychology behind such a reaction. I behaved heartlessly, reprimanded him and sent him away. Nor did I feel any regret. When the love letter I had rejected reached me again by mail, pride spread a forest fire inside of me. Thinking that Sudhakaran had deliberately disgraced me, I registered a complaint with the headmaster of our school. The headmaster immediately expelled Sudhakaran from the school in my presence. For a fleeting moment, I regretted it; at that very moment, my love for Sudhakaran attained its peak. I decided that I would write a long letter to him filled with love, repentance, heartache and sympathy and surrender myself to him as his slave. But I heard that on the very day of the dismissal, he had left home for good, taking his sister's jewels. Since then I have not heard any news about him. When I came to know from the man himself that it was he, Ramachandran, a foe of Sudhakaran, who had picked up that letter from the road where I had thrown it and mailed it to me—how can I describe the repentance and love which assailed my heart … It was *that* love letter which was in that gold case.'

Shafi was listening to her tale with the same changes of facial expression which might have occurred to Sudhakaran were he the one listening to Sarojam's story.

Two minutes of total silence. The visitor broke it: 'Do you think you will see that Sudhakaran again?'

'Can't say I won't, either.'

Shafi let out a hollow laugh.

'A man who left home seven years ago! Madam, what couldn't have happened to him? He might be begging for alms on the street, could be a labourer who just about manages to make both ends meet or he may even have died by now. If not that either, he might have become a smart thief like the one who stole your jewellery casket.'

Sarojam interrupted: 'There is no chance of him turning into a thief. He might be working in some movie production company as an actor—that is what I believe.'

The visitor laughed his hollow laugh again and said, 'Madam, why couldn't he have become a thief? Are all the thieves born thieves? Oh no! Never! Circumstances create thieves. You say that Sudhakaran stole his sister's ornaments. He might not have even dreamt of such a mean act in the wildest of his dreams that morning. Circumstances forced him to do it. When such circumstances repeat themselves, how can we presume that he would not have become a smart thief?'

Without answering, Sarojam sat with downcast eyes, lost in thought.

Shafi continued: 'Madam, let me ask you something. If you now encountered Sudhakaran as a beggar, would you receive him with the same intense love that you now feel for him?'

Sarojam's face changed. The gravity on her face of seven years ago seemed to have returned.

'Mr Shafi, you have not understood the heart of a woman.'

She rearranged her saree that had slid down from her head. 'In the years gone by Sudhakaran's stature, form and manner might have changed pathetically. But it is the same Sudhakaran of those years who would come after a game of football, face flushed and streaming sweat, with the vibrancy of youth, who is still the lord of my heart. In whichever form I might find Sudhakaran today, I cannot see him in any other way except in the image of that handsome young man of seven years ago. What if I find him as a beggar? My father has a lot of money.'

Shafi sat still like an illusionist, gazing at her without diverting his eyes. Finally he asked: 'Madam, just one more question. Let's say you met Sudhakaran as an accomplished thief. Even then? Your love for him would not falter?'

She replied in a firm and distinct voice: 'There is no bad habit that love cannot change. For the wrong that I have done to him knowingly or unknowingly—even if he were a murderer, let alone an accomplished thief—I am waiting for him with the love I have preserved within my heart ... but all your questions are irrelevant!'

Shafi suddenly turned towards Sarojam and said: 'Your Sudhakaran is here!'

'Where?' Sarojam asked, surprised.

He took off his blue-tinted glasses and put them down. He removed his hat, pulled off his false grey beard; he shed that long coat and flung it afar. With a humble smile he held Sarojam's hand and knelt before her. He raised his face to her and said: 'Sarojam, here is that old Sudhakaran. But he is a thief today. A robber who stole even *your* jewellery box. But it was not deliberate. He hadn't noticed Sarojam then. He had eyes only for the jewellery casket ... for two years, the police have been searching for him: wanted for a big case of theft. But from this moment onwards, I am not a thief; I am the servant of love.'

Sarojam looked at him from head to toe. From his pocket he produced his old love letter.

'Here—this is what put out the light in my life; it is also what lit it up now. I place it at your feet.'

She took it in her hand. Hearing the sound of boots outside, both of them strained their ears.

Inspector Narayan Singh and two constables walked into the room.

Saluting Sarojam, the inspector said, 'Miss Sarojam, we have recovered a jewellery box from a thief. Here, you can check if it is yours.'

Sarojam took the box in her hands, not feeling like saying anything out of fear.

When he turned, the inspector's eyes fell on Sudhakaran. Both of them stood glaring at each other for a long time. Abruptly, Sudhakaran took two or three steps forward and, placing his wrists together, said: 'Inspector, don't doubt it, I am the same Sudhakaran you have been looking for, who has been evading arrest for the last two years. But today I surrender myself to you. You can arrest me, handcuff me. I deserve to be punished for my deeds.'

Sarojam knelt before Sudhakaran and kissed his shackled hands. Tears welled up in her eyes, her heart throbbed. Sudhakaran and the inspector were about to leave. They reached the threshold. Slowly Sudhakaran turned and looked at Sarojam. She too was looking at him.

Sudhakaran saw the same look on her face that he had seen seven years ago when the headmaster had expelled him.

Ferry Boat
Kadavu Thoni

ONE

The dock was near the delta. There was no one in the vicinity who did not know Mammu, the ferryman. It had been seven years since he became the ferryman of the area. About twenty-five now, no one who saw his beautiful athletic form and dusky-complexioned attractive face would ever forget him.

Ever since he had begun working at the docks he had not missed a single day. The hours from dawn to midnight found him on the boat itself. He had no father or mother—just one sibling, Ayessa Umma, who was married to a Muslim bullock-cart driver who lived in the docks itself.

Mammu's dugout was his own. He had it carved out of timber with the 40 rupees he received from the capital his father had. Oh, that dugout was his only asset; it was his precious toy. He had spent seven years of his life in that little punt of his loaded with memories. It was his companion and support, the only recipient of all his love, care and his sole preoccupation. He knew not how to read or write. Still, he knew the white letters etched in the hollow of his canoe read, 'T. Mammu'. He often stood staring at those letters impassively with pride and wonder. He could scarcely believe that his boat was lifeless. How could he believe otherwise when he watched its opportune rocking, listing and pitching … its coyness?

The place where the river and the ocean meet is a very dangerous zone with whirlpools and undercurrents. Still, Mammu enjoyed letting his boat into those currents. Negotiating the menacing depths and dangerous, mysterious undercurrents and whirlpools created by the confluence of the river with the ocean had become second nature to Mammu. He had some unfailing techniques to navigate the boat through the worst of torrents without causing turbulence. He alone knew that trick.

Come gale or squall, Mammu did not hesitate to ferry the people in a hurry across the waters. If the group that ventured into the boat were his own kind, he would break into a song too. He sang well.

The owner of the wharf was Mussa Hajiyar, a businessman. He had a place in the docks itself where he traded in rice. Thereby Mammu got a daily wage from him—four anas for ferrying and one ana as rental for his canoe. Besides, if other rich businessmen came to the docks, he'd get some tips too, on the side.

Hajiyar thought highly of Mammu. When night fell he went home, leaving matters of the shop to him. The next morning Mammu would hand over the collection of the previous night to the master with nary a quarter of a paisa missing. The master would take it from him and, without so much as a glance at the money, would drop it into his pocket.

Mammu had his lunch and supper at the house of Ayessa *thatha*, for which he gave her two anas. After his supper he would go and sleep in the shack near the docks. Once a year he would go to a mosque three miles away from the docks to witness the annual consecration ceremony there. Thus, Mammu left the premises of the docks only once a year.

Seven years passed. Seven pristine years of a cool life of peace flowed by, caressing him.

TWO

It was a night in the month of Mithunam. The sky was swept clean of all the dark clouds by the incessant rains of the past many days. White silken moonlight spread a cover over the area; the sand became clarified butter and the waters an ocean of milk.

Mammu was fast asleep in his shack by the delta. All of a sudden he woke up, hearing someone call out to him. Rubbing eyes drowsy with sleep, he sat up and looked all around. A white figure appeared to be standing on the opposite bank of the river.

It was yet another eight to nine hours before dawn. Who could be calling out from the other bank at this ungodly hour? Saying that to himself he untied the rope that tethered his boat to a coconut tree; he doubled his *mundu* at the knee and pushed the canoe offshore, hopped into the stern of the dugout and began to row.

The sound of the waves lapping the cluster of rocks in the far distance sloshed in his ears. The boat slowly slithered towards the other shore, cutting through the waves bleached white by the moonlight.

His heart, now fully awake, began to sing:

'Enthinanippunkarale
Panthirandilakkunu—
Eppazhani poomaram
Virinju thaen kudikkane …'
(Oh, my beloved heart … why do you
Wait twelve years to bloom?
When will your flowering tree blossom
That I may suck its nectar.)

Mammu berthed his boat on the other shore and jumped out of it. The figure there moved away a little. He peered through the darkness at it. Suspecting it to be an apparition, he stepped back, startled.

A mother with a child on her hip.

'You must take us to the other bank—'

Those sweet words which invoked sympathy thrilled Mammu's heart. His suspicion vanished, but not his surprise. He stood staring at her unblinkingly. He could only see her face because she had covered her head with a piece of white cloth. And that face? It had the radiance of the full moon. Slender gold bangles shone on the wrist that was supporting the baby at her hip, and on her fingers glittered gold rings studded with gems. The bottom of her feet, reddened with henna, hid partially behind her pump shoes. She kept disappearing repeatedly behind a silk umbrella she held open.

Overall, she was like a female swan hidden by ripples under the tender petals of a lotus.

Except to stand and gaze at her for a very long time, Mammu could say nothing. Finally, he asked her: 'Where are you going at this unholy hour of the night?'

She lowered her head and said, 'The brilliance of the moonlight made me think it was dawn. Have to go to the railway station.'

Mammu asked no more.

She clutched the tip of the cloth she wore and raising it, took off her pump shoes, dangled them from the hand holding the child and waded towards the dugout in ankle-deep water.

Mammu got into the canoe and, with a *kuthupala*, began to scoop out the water that had sloshed into the hollow of the dugout; then he laid out a mat for the woman to sit on. The woman placed the child on the mat and drawing up her heels, squatted, slightly crouched.

Mammu dislodged the canoe from its berth and sitting on the raised stern, swung the boat toward the opposite shore and began to row leisurely. As he rowed easily with arms of steel, the little boat coursed through the bosom of the river, whose passion was roused by the touch of the moonlight. Who else was there to watch that heartening sight, except the plethora of stars twinkling in the night sky!

He experienced the taste of a new unspeakable joy. A thousand ripples of happiness made him tremulous within. He could not believe the scene he beheld before him. The darkness of midnight bathed in moonlight, the world immersed in sleep, not a sound or movement. All he heard was the distant drone of the sea which sounded like the snore of nature entrapped in sleep. His little canoe slithered through the cool bosom of the river; in it sat a pretty woman with no one for company. He wondered if she wasn't a woman of paradise who had slipped and fallen into this world.

He was ferrying her across the river … they were now midstream. Far away the waves roared as they incessantly lashed the rocks … a gentle cool breeze blew … The river licked the sides of his boat, stretching out a thousand silver tongues. That '*glaga, lagla*' sound brought a rapture to his heart. A half-moon hovered in the sky, creating a thousand silver steps in the water which lead to an unknown world of dreams. The scene was altogether surreal. A gold-tinged portrait which breathed the life of poetry!

He felt like singing but his shyness stemmed his urge.

He looked at her. Her large black eyes were resting on his face; but he was not aware of it. When their eyes met, she withdrew and sat bent over, awkwardly covering her face. That act of hers added to his discomfiture. He saw merely for a moment that face like a muskmelon born of moonlight and those eyes like the bloom of the blue lotus.

Her baby slowly crawled up to him and, holding his calf, stood up. He experienced horripilation in his heart. He looked at the child's face. It called him, '*Uppa*!' and smiled widely.

'Amina, Amina, come here!' howled the child's mother, reaching out for her. But Amina did not respond. The child just stood there hanging on to Mammu's calf.

The name Amina disconcerted Mammu. It was his mother's name.

The boat suddenly lurched and shook. The little child might have toppled over—but before that, Mammu clasped it firmly between his legs. Amina burst out laughing and began to slap Mammu's thighs. Mammu bent down and picked up the child and seated it on his lap, holding her with one arm while rowing the boat with the other.

Amina resumed her antics seated in his lap, scratching his chin, pinching his lips. Mammu was seized with emotion. He repeatedly kissed Amina on her full little lips and her chubby cheeks.

'Doesn't Amina have a father?' asked Mammu.

'No,' answered the young woman in a melancholy tone. 'It's been three months since he passed away. The child is taking to you so fondly because she thinks you are her *uppa*!'

Mammu kissed the child once more. It giggled aloud like the waves and shoved its little fingers into his mouth. His heart drowned in ecstasy. He let out a sigh.

The canoe advanced resolutely.

Mammu looked at the distant ocean. The vast ocean looked contiguous with the sky in the light of the moon. He looked at the opposite bank of the river and saw a star falling into the coconut grove, twinkling. He looked at the young woman's face. She too sat watching the same star.

The boat was nearing the shore. He picked up the child from his lap and kissing it once more, placed it down.

The boat hadn't quite come to standstill. As the woman stepped forward to gather her child, the boat rocked and tilted to one side and she pitched forward—towards Mammu—and Mammu's arm encircled her and saved her from falling. All this happened in a flash. She leapt backwards instantly with a tremor!

Mammu couldn't help but stand there dazed with a frozen emotion that was new to him.

The young woman got off the boat, placed the child on the ground and untying the knotted end of the cloth she wore, reached out three-quarters of an ana to Mammu.

To collect a fare was his duty, wasn't it—he took the money from her.

She picked up the child, turned back to look at Mammu with an expression of farewell and walked away.

That she was going away alone at that unholy hour caused much anguish to Mammu. Yet he could not find the courage to follow her. He stood there for a long time watching the path she took. The rooster crowed. As if awakened from a dream, he walked over to his dugout and sat in it. Suddenly he saw something glittering in the boat and walked over to check. There, on the mat that the woman had sat on, was a gold bangle. He picked it up and hopped onto land. He ran after her following the route she had taken. After running a whole mile, he spotted her at a distance.

When Mammu approached her, running and panting from behind, she inadvertently let out a cry. But when he held out that gold bangle, blurting out a couple of incoherent words through his gasping and stood before her nervously, she brightened up.

'Is it still a long way to the railway station?'

'Another two miles.'

Then with trepidation, he spoke the words that he wanted to, even at the berthing point of the canoe: 'If you do not know the route, I could show you the way.'

She consented happily.

It was a broad sandy by-lane. Moonlight merged with sand that looked like powdered glass. Henna plants grew wild on the high fences on either side of the lane. *Arippa chedi* and *thechi maram*, usually found in the country side, lay entangled with each other. In that deep tranquility the two of them walked on that lonely path, making small talk. The cool morning breeze blew past, caressing them.

Amina, perched on the woman's hip, was struggling to get over to Mammu. Mammu reached out for her. The woman handed the child over to him.

From a gooseberry tree nearby a dove and a *pullu* began to chirp, announcing the advent of dawn.

They were approaching the railway station. Mammu handed Amina back to the woman with great reluctance, ending their conversation that way: 'Where do you have to go?'

'Kozhikode.'

'Whom do you have there?'

'*Elappa*.'

'Where in Kozhikode?'

'In the city itself.'

'When will you return?'

'Not in the near future.'

Silence for a long time.

And then she said: 'I am thankful for all the help you gave me. Will you be coming to Kozhikode sometime?'

Mammu stood thinking. Then he said in a voice filled with sadness: 'Who will mind the ferry if I go?'

Again, silence. Then in a subdued, cracked voice and with great hesitation: 'Your name?'

She stood for a while nervously without speaking. Mammu's face flushed.

Then she uttered softly, 'Aleema'.

'Aleema, Aleema!' Mammu repeated to himself.

They were now very near the railway station. 'There is the booking office; I must go now. The hawkers with their headloads must be waiting at the dock for me.' Aleema looked once more at Mammu's departing form, her glance full of compassion and yearning.

Mammu's heart soared like a buoyant tender bud of coconut straining to stay afloat in water. He walked on, head bowed, without turning to look. After a few steps he couldn't help but turn back. With an emotion steeped in anxiety, he looked. Aleema was standing there without taking her eyes off him. When their eyes met, she held Amina's little hands and beckoned to him playfully.

Mammu hurried on to the docks.

The headload workers had been howling for the ferry from the opposite bank. He dislodged his dugout from its perch on the shore. But contrary to his usual style, he did not hop jauntily into the canoe. He did not sing while rowing. His arms worked the oars mechanically.

It was light and the moon had vanished like a bubble. When his boat crossed the midpoint of the river the third time, the thundering sound of the train running over the bridge assailed his ears. The train rushing towards Kozhikode, carrying her!

He sat silently, eyes wide open.

THREE

From that day onwards, Mammu's nature changed completely. Gone was his jubilance. No more songs and jokes. He no longer joined in the frivolity of the people he ferried. He spoke to no one. He spent all his time brooding.

New desires and schemes sprouted in his mind. Fresh ripples of joyful tunes of a song came from afar and embraced him. He was engrossed in many unforgettable sweet memories. Some live dreams loomed before his eyes.

This melancholy and depression in Mammu did not go unnoticed by Hajiyar.

'*Entha, nyammante Mammune oru konakkedu?*' (What is the matter with our Mammu?) Hajiyar once asked him, for which Mammu had no answer.

Three days passed. On the morning of the fourth day, with a sorrowful face, Mammu approached Hajiyar bashfully. Hajiyar studied his pale, tired and emaciated body closely.

Handing over the collection of the previous day, Mammu said: '*Mothalali nyammante thoni vanganam.*' (Master must buy my boat.)

Hajiyar was stunned.

'*Entha, Mammunnu paisekku muttundo?*' (Does Mammu need money?)

'*Alla, nyamma ponu.*' (No, I am leaving.)

'*Engittu?*' (Where to?)

'*Kozhikkotteku.*' (To Kozhikode.)

'*Enthinu?*' (Why?)

No answer.

Hajiyar asked many other things. But Mammu merely stood there, head bowed in sorrow.

Finally, Hajiyar opened his box and took out a ten-rupee and a five-rupee note and gave them to Mammu. That kind-hearted master gave him five anas as wages for the previous day and an additional one rupee as a gift.

Mammu left with tears in his eyes. Gripping the money tightly, lacking the courage to look at his beloved dugout one last time, Mammu walked head bowed, straight to the railway station.

By noon, he arrived at Kozhikode. That new city frightened him. Apart from the surroundings he had grown up in, Mammu had not seen even a small town. Seeing the teeming crowds, the play of opulence, the incessant flow of vehicles, the exquisite buildings, other fascinating scenes of wonderment and the latest fashion in clothes, he was wonderstruck. He stood cowering like a fly which had fallen into a frothing mug of brew.

He stepped onto the vacant patio of a shop to take rest. A beggar with a festering, stinking wound on his foot also climbed onto that patio. Mammu quickly stepped down.

The dust and the noise of the city bothered him. The stench of rot and the swarms of flies repulsed him.

He did not feel hungry. Still for the sake of it, he felt he must have his lunch. Someone pointed out a big hotel to him. He went in and sat down for his meal. 10 to 12 cups and bowls were lined up before him. He managed to eat a handful of rice without even touching the array of dishes, got up and washed his hands. A group of workers in the hotel ridiculed him and sniggered at him.

Charges for a midday meal: eight anas.

He felt the need for a new set of clothes. He stepped into the first clothing store that he saw. The fellows in the shop cajoled and persuaded him to buy clothes and other stuff for six rupees. He began to loiter in the city, wearing a new dress with a green belt and cap and a handkerchief among other things.

Mammu did not understand anything. No familiar faces. No one to explain matters to him. That poor fellow searched for someone on the playgrounds and on the beaches and in all the lanes. He stared blankly at the verandahs of innumerable buildings. He saw plenty of beautiful faces, but he did not find *that* particular beautiful face. That huge city had swallowed it wholly. He wandered about in vain, searching for it.

To sleep that night too, he had to depend on a hotel. But he did not sleep a wink. Pounding from outside and the mosquitoes and his own thoughts from within tormented him. He tried rolling over and sleeping on his side and back again for a long time. At last, he sat up on his mat. He spent time staring into that darkness till it dawned.

This way he languished for 15 days! The last paisa he had with him was spent. That night he slept on an empty stomach with a smoked and charred brain on the patio of a wayside shop, resting his head in the crook of his arm.

FOUR

Hajiyar had locked up his shop and gone home long ago. It was past midnight. There came a figure shuffling slowly towards the docks.

It appeared like nothing else but a ghost. That pale, emaciated, lean and dishevelled form stood beside the shack near the dock. It looked around in all four directions.

Though the rain had stopped, the sky was not yet clear. As the moon had emerged from behind the veil of the clouds, a faint moonlight had spread all around. The place looked like what was left of a smudged old painting in the pale light of the moon.

The river was rushing with a current driven by emotion. The rain clouds began to float from west to east in a cluster. From among that group, a couple of stars looked down with their eyes wide open. A terrible quiet pervaded the area, heralding the onset of a violent storm.

That figure looked all around warily once more.

At a slightly raised spot, a little farther away from the docks, that dugout lay tethered to a coconut tree. The figure reached there within the snap of a finger.

That little canoe, probably because it recognized him, swayed and wobbled with coyness in the rippling water and in a very slow coquettish way began to glide towards him. Who could say that it didn't have a life of its own?

That entity held the raised stern of the boat and sighed. It looked at the white inscription on the hollowed interior of the dugout and its eyes filled with tears. Mammu had become three-quarters of a spectre. He had been walking without rest for 50 miles. It had been two days since his last meal. His shirt and cloth were smeared with red dust.

He cast a glance at the shack by the dock. On its parapet burned a tin lamp. On the mat on the floor slept a huge fat Muslim using a metal trunk for a pillow and snoring loudly.

Mammu was only too well aware of his plight. That dugout was no longer his. He had no claims on the docks. To cross the river if he must, he too had to spend three-quarters of an ana. He looked at that Muslim with jealousy and indignation. Where had this creature sprung from?

The roar of the waves rang out relentlessly. The sight of a thousand dancing ripples sipping with a '*glagala*' sound, the light of the waxing moon falling on the surface of that river with its strong undercurrents, thrilled his heart. He looked at the dark shadows of the hutments and the coconut groves on the opposite bank of the river in that hoary backdrop.

He slowly got into the boat. Bending over, he scooped out all the water that had collected inside it with the *kuthupala*. Then he untied the tether of the boat, pushed it offshore and seated in it, his legs outstretched, began to row westward aiming for the sea.

A new light flashed in his heart. His thoughts came to life and turned into a lively song.

'Enthinanippunkarale
Panthirandilakkunu—
Eppazhani poomaram
Virinju thaen kudikkane …'

Frolicking in waves of joy, he sang that song over and over again.

The speed of the canoe increased. The uninterrupted deafening roar of the waves came nearer and nearer. It seemed to beckon to him invitingly. The sky darkened; the wind began to blow with great force. The whole sea, with its frothing waves rising, looked like milk boiling over. The boat shot forward towards the spot where the river and the sea fused in embrace.

Mammu dropped the oar, and holding both the edges of the boat, smiled softly and looked with opaque eyes at the vast expanse in front of him, from which rose a defiant roar of challenge. With two leaps, the boat shot up and dropped again at a distance. It was time to transit. A huge wave growled its peremptory welcome to Mammu.

As each wave struck those rocks with force, like a charging lion roaring and waggling its greying mane, a thousand pearls scattered in all four directions.

The boat bobbed and yawed as it covered another short distance. The next moment, a serpentine wave with its rearing hood and hiss, rose above it and swiped it backwards …

The next day, the new ferryman, Moossahaji ran up to the master and spluttered: 'Master, in the terrible storm of last night, our boat cut loose and floated away.'

Hajiyar looked at him silently.

On the Bank of the River

Nadeetheerathil

Along the base of a barren hillock that resembled an *Aeenthalchacka* snaked a small river. The drooping branches of huge trees, smaller trees and tangled creepers almost hid its banks—a dreadful darkness hung over that place.

Not far from there was a deep spot in the middle of the stream where the bedrock lay submerged—'*Thalavetti Para*' is what the old timers called it. It is said that this was the spot where, in old times, convicts were beheaded. Nobody bathed there. The water in that part of the stream was discoloured.

Beside the hillock, amid the vines and creepers, rose a withered date palm. At its top was a fruit that looked like a flame; the fragrance that emanated from it pervaded the surroundings. Near the date palm stood alone a *kammati maram* with a portion of it wilted and drooping like a partially paralyzed patient. On its branches hung five or six parcels of old mats which reflected in the mouldy water of the stream. They were the hides of goats and cattle wrapped in mats and hung to drip-dry. Next to it grew a thick red denuded tap root, resembling the palm of a leper, with all the mud under it gone, powdering and disintegrating away. All around a *pulakkalli maram*, with all its leaves shed and inclined like the skeletal formation on the chest of a horse, grew wild plantain trees looking like the reared hoods of snakes.

From somewhere among those thickets, rising straight up to the sky, stood a huge *ayanippilavu*. A brook that was almost dry joined the stream further down beyond the deep part of the river. That area was a berthing bay for boats.

It was mid noon. The sand on the bank of the rivulet had begun to scorch as the blazing sun beat down on it.

Madhavi amma, having bathed her son, dried him, wiped his face clean, combed his hair and put on his red silken *konakam* and sent him back to the shore. That six-year-old sat on a rock with his legs outstretched before him under a teak tree like an obedient boy. Five minutes passed. His limbs began to move one by one gradually. Childhood is a *rasabindu*. It cannot remain static.

The child's wide-open eyes fluttered around restlessly. He checked to see if he had all the fingers on his hand. He measured the length of his forehead, nose and chin with his forefinger. Then he closed one nostril and began to hum, tapping the other softly. He played the fiddle this way for some time before stopping. Then he pressed the pits of the upper eyelids with his fingers and, squinting his eyes, looked around at the trees and plants and thrilled to see them double. Then suddenly he had a brainwave.

'*Ammae* … shall I play making dams in the brook?'

'No, no, darling! Don't play in the dirt. Unni, you just sit there quietly. And—careful you don't lose that ring!—'

Unni pulled a face. He picked up the ring placed on his thigh. A red gem-encrusted gold ring. His mother had entrusted it to him till she finished her bath.

He tried the ring on each of his fingers, finally slipping it on his right thumb. Not knowing what to do next, he sat with his arms crossed in front of him and eyes shut tight. Then he opened his eyes and tried to touch the tip of his nose with his tongue; he filled his mouth with air and hissed like a snake. Thus he went on teaching himself several yoga exercises.

'The sun is beating down on me. *Ammae*, shall I go and sit in the shade under the bamboo clump?' He called out to his mother.

'Um …' Madhavi amma hummed, lost in thought, washing clothes.

He moved over to the shade of the bamboo cluster, imitating the limp of an invalid. This way he managed a cover from the watch of his mother.

Along the bamboo cluster flowed a little rivulet. The midday sun reflected on the water collected in a pit in that trickle. A dragonfly frisked over the water, rising and suddenly dipping to skim the surface of the water only to rise again.

This caught Unni's attention. Slanting his neck and squinting at the scene, he began to rise slowly.

A very pretty dragonfly, it was. A little fly that wore a red thong like himself. He knew a trick to make the dragonfly pick up tiny pebbles. Before he had taken two steps forward, the fly gave up its water sport and flew past him onto a *thechi* plant and perched on it. Stretching his hand with his forefinger and thumb curved like a pair of tongs, he crouched warily towards the *thechi* bush. Before he could get closer, the dragonfly flew away eastward without pausing.

Unni did not give up. With determination he set out to seek the dragonfly. He sighted it rising from an *aripoo*, a wild flower with tiny petals in a shrub. He crawled into the shrubbery. By the time he extended his hand the dragonfly flew off the wild plant and settled on a branch of the *kammati* tree. In the next instant it flew off again and descended on the leaf of a plantain tree, as if paying obeisance to it. Cursing the insolence of the fly, Unni waited with his hand still poised, naughty eyes narrowed and mouth agape, waiting for the dragonfly to settle down. The fly rose again and flew back to the same tree and perched there.

The sun shone through the sprawling branches of the *ayinippilavu* onto the thicket, beaming a circle of light into it. In it could be seen clearly the *eenthalchacka*, the skeleton of the *pulakkalli* and the old mat packets dangling from the *kammati* tree.

There was a movement in the burrow at the base of the *ayinippilavu*. The dry leaves nearby shifted and rustled. An eight-foot cobra slowly slithered out of the burrow and wrapped itself around the withered trunk of the tree and withdrew to the other side.

The fly was taking a long respite on the branch of the *kammati* tree next to the *eenthalchacka*. Unni's tender hands were slowly moving towards it. His very soul was lodged on that branch. All he could see in this universe was the red tail of that dragonfly.

Sunshine like molten silver fell on his fingers. Seeing the sparkling gem embedded on his ring, a pair of small eyes like red crystal beads shone from behind the *eenthalchacka*. The snake lay still, enjoying the fragrance of the *eenthalchacka*. The glimmer of the gemstone on the ring attracted it. It slowly raised its head, eyes gleaming, and with an intake of air into its body, rippled all over, swelled a bit, spread open and reared its hood.

The dragonfly had not moved. Unni's hand lowered and advanced evenly. Abruptly, the fly flapped its wings, rose a little, circled around a couple of times and settled back on the same spot. It seemed reluctant to leave the circle of light cast by the brilliant midday sun.

The cobra remained still, watching the ring. The raised little fingers curled like tongs seemed to have frozen in midair.

Unni's fingers began to move most cautiously. This time, not straight ahead; with a change in childish strategy, they were encircling the fly. His hand was moving right towards the mouth of the serpent. Along with the gradual motion of his hand, following the sparkle of the gemstone, the snake's hood twisted and turned. As the gem approached it, the cobra reared its hood further back, poised to strike.

The dragonfly was motionless, stupefied by the sunlight. The little fingers were merely a mustard seed's girth away from the fly … a moment's silence … the fingers clasped like the batting of an eyelid. The tail of the dragonfly that looked like the burnt end of a leaf frond was trapped between those fingers in an instant; the dragonfly flailed its wings in a bid to escape. Unni spun around like greased lightning and disappeared, bellowing in triumph.

The eight-foot cobra, taken aback, twisted its hood all around, like a rubber toy. Then it sheepishly retracted its hood, turned its head and slithered down, flicking its tongue in and out. It sniffed at the mat sacks dangling from the *kammati* tree … the serpent again deflected its head and moved across the ground, entwined around the tap root that looked like the palm of a leper and, coiling around the base of the *pulakkalli* tree, advanced south through the clump of plantain trees.

Night Queen Flower
[Nishagandhi]

The fragrance of the *nishagandhi* is the one I love most. There is nothing else that attracts me as much as the sweet scent that rises from the blossoming petals of this plant known as the 'Night Queen' in English. The fresh fragrance that wafts from the flora growing on fences, the corners of gardens and from behind walls, creeps towards me in the dark and intoxicates my inner self. The Night Queen is a prostitute among flowers—sleeping through the day, she stalks in the darkness after dusk and embraces people unawares, ensnaring them. Yes, that mesmerizing scent is ideal to a whore!

But in my own garden, I will never let *nishagandhi* grow. In my beautiful garden, resplendent with a variety of flowers, you will never find a single plant of it, for which there is a specific reason and an old story behind it ...

I was then a seventeen-year-old college student. In the life of a young man, the seventeenth year is a dangerous phase. Although the British call it, 'sweet seventeen,' I have named it, 'fatal seventeen!' At the onset of a heady newness, he will experience many desires which lead to unnecessary love tangles, he will chase the novel ideologies he hears only to end up eating dust; he will worship secretly all the good-looking girls whom he deifies and finally wander around disappointed—a harmless daydreamer. Editors have suffered much due to these seventeen-year-olds, because it is an age when even the most dumb-witted will find the inspiration to write poetry. He will be averse to becoming a proponent of materialism and tend to be a philosopher of spirituality. The route that his amour takes will also be likewise. More than the love story in '*Vilasalatika*,' he would prefer the tales of love expounded in '*Nalini*' or '*Leela*.' The Italian, Dante, would be his ideal lover.

With neither their knowledge, much less their permission, having researched the beauty, character and love interests of several girls, the girl who finally had the good fortune of qualifying to become my 'Ideal Girl,' was Malati—a high school student. A fair-skinned girl, slightly plump, not too tall with a broad figure; she had perfectly round breasts and a face like the waxing moon. It was her dreamy eyes which attracted me at first. Overall, there was an aura of beauty about her. 'Malu' was a serious little girl who seldom smiled. I liked her gravitas immensely. That's the way a girl ought to be. Those days, I despised girls who pranced around giggling and frolicking. Every evening I would take my place on the upstairs verandah of my building, eagerly waiting to watch the grand ceremony of her walking along the side of the road like a little swan, head bowed, pressing a heavy load of books against her bosom, in a coarse green skirt and white khadar blouse dotted with red, dangling an umbrella in her hand with a handle shaped like a cashew fruit without its nut. Little did she know that I worshipped her day and night. I put away the logarithms and cotangents and the homework filled with conundrums of our mathematics professor, Ramanatha Iyer, and began to write poetry about Malati: of the way she walked and her stack of books—

'Koonkanakke valarnuvarum maru
Kankayente karalum kariyunnu ...'
(At the sight of her cone-shaped breasts
My heart burns to cinder.)

'*Bhesh!*' (Fantastic!) I myself liked those lines very much. Though I did write the poem thus, I was determined that I wouldn't objectify her in my thoughts. A divine love based on lofty ideology! All the same it must contain some pathos and disappointment. I prayed for an opportunity to wander about in disappointment, singing spiritual songs, like Madanan, who failed in love. I fantasized about Malu sagging onto my shoulder like '*kethuvil thanu pattiya pathaka polave …*' (a drooping flag that drapes itself around the flag mast).

Malati lived in a big house on a large plot located about two furlongs to the west of our house. Her father and I went no further than cursory greetings. I doubt whether Malati, who always walked with her head bowed, had even seen my face.

I would go for a stroll after dinner. A ridge on the fields that led away from the road ended at an 'elephant door' on the west side of her house. Four yards away from it was a shrub of the *nishagandhi* plant that grew as tall as a man. I discovered that if I squatted behind that shrub, I could see Malati through a slit in her window, seated in her room reading.

The light from a table lamp clearly showed the changes in her expression. She wore a blouse that exposed her breasts partially. Because her luxurious hair that fell over her breasts covered the blouse, a portion of her fair breast looked like a waterfall pouring out from the crevices of rocks. Spreading her English Reader on the table before her, bending over slightly and supporting her forehead with a left hand, she would begin to read—no, chant. That girl did not have the habit of reading aloud. '*And Seetha wanted to go with Rama*'—she would mutter at times, for the benefit of no one in particular. On and on she would read till she felt sleepy. As the depth of her sleep increased, her head would sink lower and lower like the pan of a balance and touch the table softly, whereupon, she would break her 'journey to Vaikunth,' raise her head and look around to check her whereabouts. Then she would sit, looking out through that slit in the window into the darkness outside for a long time. Watching all this from my hiding place in the thicket and with the surge of sympathy I felt, I would feel tempted to yell, 'Darling, that will do; now go to bed!' But after rubbing her eyes for a long time, she would resume reading. I would stand there with bated breath, looking at the deity of my heart impassively. At such times, the intoxicating fragrance of the *nishagandhi* plant would enter my being and waft down into my heart. Every moment I spent in that fragrant thicket drove me to ecstasy. Like a heavenly dream seen in a sweetly scented siesta, that gem of a girl would go on frolicking before me ... the redolence of the *nishagandhi* seemed to stick to every thought and dream of mine.

Sometimes she read Malayalam poetry, reciting the '*Manjari*' beautifully.

'*Ammakkumathramallarkume chenneduthummavaikkan thonnumallo ...*'

(Not just the mother, but anyone would want to cuddle and kiss ...)

Haa! Those lines had to be heard as she sang them ... and ... one could not but yearn to kiss *her* own lips.

This way, without break, for three months I sat hidden in that *nishagandhi* shrubbery for an hour every night, worshipping her silently. The fragrance of *nishagandhi* and the beauty of Malati's face adhered to my mind. I enjoyed a fragrant, heavenly beauty day after delightful day.

The rainy season had begun. *Thiruvathira Njatthuvela* had set in after Idavapathi.

The drenching rain was no obstacle to my trips to the shrubs in Malati's compound. But often, when the rains became heavy, she would shut that window. *Oh no*! Along with that would shut the door to my own heart. I would return home disappointed and rain-soaked, gloomy and heavy-hearted.

One day as I sat hidden in that bush, I overheard her father tell her brother: 'Tomorrow we must cut and prune all the plants in the garden and bury them. There are some shrubs also in the compound growing wild; we must get rid of them too.'

My heart caught fire. In their attempt to clear their garden and compound by chopping off branches, pruning the sprigs of overgrown plants and planting the cut twigs to take root, they were sure to cut down that *nishagandhi* foliage too. That plant had spread and grown too tall and tangled. If my love nest was wrecked, what would become of me? All my pleasures and dreams were invested there—like a bird with its nest ruined, where would I go? What scheme then to have a glimpse of that face in serene solitude?

There seemed no option. I decided then that the only course left was to write a letter to Malati asking her to protect that *nishagandhi* plant.

That night I thought it over till it was three in the morning and compiled a missive as follows:

Lady of my heart,

It is now three months since I have been hiding in that nishagandhi shrub every night to worship you from afar; it was my desire to spend years like that being a silent admirer without letting anyone—not even you—know. But, 'Vidhivihitham evanum lankhichu koodumo?' (Can anyone deflect his own share of Fate?) Haa! Can't even imagine it! That thicket is going to be destroyed by your father tomorrow. That will break my penance. This letter is to request you to save that thicket and 'yours truly' from that calamity. If such a pristine and selfless love scheme of mine must be preserved, your kind attention is my only recourse—Om Shanti!

Rest later,
Slave of your love.
(Sd.)

In order to reach the letter as soon as possible to Malati, I set out for her house very early in the morning. On the pretext of asking for a white 'Prince of Wales' plant, I entered her compound. There was a commotion there. Five to ten people from the neighborhood stood in front of her house. I edged my way into their midst and peeked.

A horrendous snake was sprawled there, beaten to death. It was at least three feet long.

A first-rate cobra!

'The fellow was living in that sweet-smelling bush over there. When we cleared the thicket we found a huge burrow. As we began to pound the opening, he shot out! What is surprising is that, in spite of it being holed up there all this time, none of us knew it.' The elderly carpenter who had thrashed it dead looked at me and, placing a finger on his nose, said: 'Just look at him! All dots and checks!'

Then, seeing the tail of the snake wiggle like the hand of the electric meter in the telegraph office, the *ashari* (carpenter) perked up: 'Why, hasn't the bloke died yet?' He began to beat the snake again with the dried stalk of a coconut frond that he held in his hand. The head of the snake was smashed and splattered blood.

I stayed no longer. I do not know how I got back home. The more I thought about that incident, the more I felt like someone was shoveling embers on to my heart. Whenever I recalled that a terrible snake was coiled beside me with its mouth wide open, enjoying the fragrance of that plant while I sat there in the dark enjoying divine beauty, I thought I would go insane with terror.

Much as I tried, I could not wipe out the mental image of a cobra rearing its hood behind me as I sat entranced.

That very night I developed a fever which rose higher and higher. I began to see many frightful dreams and became delirious. I saw snakes wherever I looked—on the canopy frame of the bed, on the box rearing its hood, several slithering in through a slit between the panels of the window; another dangling upside down right next to me—

'*Ayyo*! Snake! Snake!' I cried out. The people at home came rushing with sticks and searched everywhere. I sat up, startled that a snake was trying to rest its hood on my shoulder from behind.

During such hallucinations, I would see Malati with a girl's face and the body of a snake, a serpent-woman. I, who enjoyed seeing her face, was terror-stricken at the sight of her body.

I lay in bed for a month with fever. Then my illness alleviated. When I went out for a walk, I saw at the entrance of Malati's house a board hung that proclaimed, 'For rent'. Upon enquiry I learnt that the family had shifted to Kannur a week ago to which place her father had been transferred.

I never saw Malati again. Recently I heard that she was married and had two children. Just a week ago I picked up my letter to her from among many others I had preserved—and destroyed it.

Whenever the redolence of the *nishagandhi* wafts through the air, delectable old memories of the insane love of my seventeenth year rise in my mind. Through that fragrance I visualize the face of a girl studying sleepily—and the raised hood of a cobra, simultaneously. It is because of that nameless fear that there is no *nishagandhi* in my garden.

Mad Dog
Bhrandan Naya

Even after two hours of daybreak, Keeran was curled up on the mat without getting up, covered snugly with his own *mundu*. He had woken up long ago. Under that thick soiled cloth he lay motionless with his eyes wide open like a frog.

After half an hour, he got up slowly and, flapping the dust off the *mundu*, wore it around his waist. Then he coughed a couple of times and stepped down into the courtyard and looked all around.

Keeran's very old mother, wizened and greyed—surely over ninety—crouched in the courtyard blinking, like an owl cast into sunshine. His six-year-old son was pacing the length of the courtyard with a raised stick in one hand and a coir rope in the other, its end tied to the dried spathe of a coconut frond, at the tip of which he had driven in two small sticks, pretending it was an ox that he was droving, producing strange sounds, talking to himself and shaking his head.

His eyes darted towards the vast expanse of fields that spread out before their hut. The paddy fields, which lay bare after the first harvest, had not yet been tilled for the next sowing. The paddy he received (as wages) after the harvest was all finished. It had been two days since water had been boiled to cook rice.

His *cherumi* groaned from inside the hut pathetically—she was in an advanced stage of pregnancy. The symptoms showed that she would deliver either that day or the next. But all Keeran had was a discarded quarter of an ana and little else. Keeran looked at the fields once more. The void there permeated his thoughts. He had nothing to do, nowhere to go.

Keeran slowly moved towards the fields. He bent over a '*attamkazha*' there and scooped water in his cupped hands from the irrigation ditch and washed his face, rinsed his mouth a couple of times and spat, stuck his forefinger in his mouth and ran it over his teeth both ways, rinsed his mouth once more, raised the loose end of his *mundu* and wiped his face; then he stepped on to the ridge in the field and headed for the road.

When he reached the road he was attracted to an unusual crowd that had gathered in front of a shop. He stood at a distance from the gathering with his mouth agape in childish curiosity. He listened to the conversation between Raman Nair and Ali Mappila.

'Hey, Raman Nair, why have people gathered in front of Kandakuruppu's shop?'

'Oh that? You know that reddish-coloured dog of Chappunni Nair? It turned mad yesterday and bit four or five dogs and a cow last night. This morning it bit the washerman Kelu's son too. Kelu is here to take a certificate from the village headman to take his son to the hospital.'

'Why is the headman's certificate needed?'

'If one is bitten by a rabid dog, he gets five or six anas a day for both transport and to cover the expenses at the hospital.'

Ali Mappila forced his way into their midst. Kelu sat with his son on his lap, gazing blankly at everybody, not knowing what to do when bitten by a mad dog.

'*Keluo*, go right now to the *adhikari*'s house with your son; he will be at home.' Chandan, who stood there with a basket of vegetables on his head, advised Kelu. Kelu carried the child on his shoulder and walked towards the headman's house. The crowd dispersed; Keeran also turned back.

He reached Karuppan's tea shop. He squatted on the roadside and called out: 'Daa—*arachaya*! Half a glass of tea!'

After 10 minutes the tea-stall owner placed a glass of tea before Keeran and said: 'I have added enough sugar and tea leaves; if you bicker, you'll get nothing, you hear?'

First he would order '*aapu chaya*'. When served half a glass of tea he would say, '*Kaduppam thone ayippoyi … itthri chaya thanni*!' (The tea is too strong, give me some stock.)

When the stock of the brew was poured, he would say, in the dialect of an illiterate: '*Madhurolya, Embrane…*' (It's not sweet, Sir …)

Complaining so, he would make the stall owner add sugar to his stock. Thus Keeran knows the trick to convert an '*aapu chaya*' into a full glass of tea. Karuppan too was wise to this gimmick. In these times when the price of tea and sugar have shot up, don't anyone dare play such pranks on Karuppan!

Keeran, who was disturbed by the words of the tea-stall owner, blew into his glass a couple of times, cupping it with both hands, and swallowed a mouthful. Each time he gulped down some tea, he would waggle his head for no reason at all. Having drunk a quarter glass, he put it down and peered greedily at the pancakes stacked on a seared leaf placed on a table in the shop.

He wanted a '*kadi*', a bite of something, very badly. But the matter of payment was a problem. Anyway he decided to test his luck.

'*Oreendu pathiri … pathireente aachu naalellu.*' (A piece of *pathiri*, but you will get the cash only tomorrow.)

The last sentence was spoken in a very subdued voice.

'*Paisa illengee, pathireem thinnanda.*' (No money? Then don't eat any *pathiri*.) The stall owner said, stirring another glass of tea noisily with a spoon, '*Neeyu vegam chaya kudichu glass ozhikkada* … hmm' (Finish that tea soon and free the glass, you …!)

Keeran grinned sheepishly and sipped the last drop remaining in the glass. Then he frisked out the quarter of an ana coin from his armpit and pushed it before him along with the empty glass and got up.

For a long time he strolled around listlessly on that road. An hour passed. Keeran saw even from a distance Kelu returning from the headman's house. Curious to know the outcome of Kelu's trip, Keeran stood in his path, on the ridge.

'*Adhikaryambrane kandu thattipeettu kityo?*' Keeran called out. (Did you get the certificate from the *adhikari*, the headman?)

'Yes, I did! I did! Now I'm headed straight for the hospital.'

'*Puthanenthu kityekkum?*' (How much money would you get?)

'Maybe six anas a day, I think. I believe injections are needed for 21 days.' Kelu said as he walked on without pausing to turn back.

Keeran again stepped down into the field. As he walked, head bowed, through that vast desolate field, images of six anas and a mad dog kept whirling in his brain.

He reached his hovel quite late that night. Through the day nobody there had had even a drop of water or a meal with any substance in it. At dusk, his sick and pregnant wife had gone into the neighboring compound and cut some fleshy stalks of an edible leaf and some pulses and, making a boiled meal of it, had gone to sleep.

Before dawn the next day, the *cherumi* woke up to the cries of her son and the *cheruman* yelling '*Ayyo, Prandannai* …' (*Ayyo*, mad dog …)

Keeran was running around the hut holding a staff. He came bounding to his *cherumi*: 'Our son sleeping on the verandah has been bitten by a mad dog!'

Cherumi looked intently at *cheruman*'s face. His teeth were stained with blood. *Cherumi* asked in surprise and suspicion: '*Ngala pallimmelendaa chora*?' (Why is there blood on your teeth?)

Keeran, alarmed, swiftly wiped off the stains with the loose end of his *mundu*.

'*Mindalledi, pandare …!*' (Don't you utter a word, you worthless slut …!)

Cherumi went to check the child. He was bleeding from his heel. He was wailing. But he himself did not know what had happened.

Hearing the yowling and howling of Keeran, some people in the neighborhood and a few passers-by came running. Keeran explained to each of them tactfully, in a voice filled with despair and fear, how the mad dog had come and bitten his child and run off into the pineapple grove.

A reddish dog, tail tucked between its hind legs. Mouth open and tongue sticking out, froth trickling down from it; it staggered as it ran and was panting heavily—that was the description Keeran gave of the dog.

'Certainly, a mad dog!' Milkman Kanaran confirmed. 'It must be Chappunni Nair's dog. Heard someone say that it bit the washerman Kelu's son too, yesterday.'

'It must not be allowed to live. Must be beaten to death on sight,' said toddy tapper Chathu angrily. 'Which way did the blighter run, *Keera*?'

'*Adiyanoru nokke kandullu … Pinne chaithaneppole engotto oru marachilu.*' (The underling [himself]) merely had a glimpse of it; then it vanished like a ghost.)

The adhikari's first auspicious vision of the day when he came to the verandah on waking, was Keeran slouching at a distance, humbly covering his mouth with a hand, carrying his son on his shoulders.

When Keeran saw the *adhikari* on the verandah, he pinched the child's leg and told him softly, '*Nelolicheda*!' (Cry, fellow ...!)

Chathan began to wail.

'Why have you come, *cheruman*?' the *adhikari* shouted across to Keeran.

'*Adiyante chekkane pranthannaya kadichambrane—nheem* …!' (A mad dog bit the underling's son, my lord!)

Keeran also began to cry.

'And did you beat the dog to death?'

'*Naya panyanyi, thamrane* …' (The dog ran away, my lord …)

'*Bha*! You donkey! Did you just stand there and watch it go? Which dog was it?'

'*Chappunni thamrante chopannaya.*' (The red dog of the landlord Chappunni.)

'The one that bit the washerman's son yesterday?'

'*Addu anne, thamraane* …' (The same one, my lord …)

'What kind of worthless people these local fellows are! Scum … who can't even kill a rabid dog!'

The headman sat on the parapet of the veranda, muttering.

'What on earth must I do for you now?'

'*Chattippeettu.*' (Certificate.)

The *adhikari* gave him a certificate that said that Keeran's son was bitten by a mad dog that morning. Carrying Chathan over his shoulder, Keeran rushed to the hospital in the town without wasting time.

An uncouth chap who looked like a *paalakkolu* stuck a needle near the navel of the boy and injected the medicine while Keeran held him down; the child shrieked in pain.

That day Keeran returned to his hut in a state of joy. On his head was a pound of rice wrapped in a coarse towel, a bunch of raw bananas over it; in his hand was fish slung on a string, and on his shoulder was a weak and spent Chathan resting his tired head. Of the money he had received from the hospital for expenses, he had spent just one ana at the toddy shop.

By the fourth injection administered to him, Chathan's body began to swell. He could neither get up nor walk. Still Keeran, with great discipline, without break, would support the child and haul him to the hospital. He proudly proclaimed to all he met on the way that his son had been bitten by a mad dog and that '*Adhikari Thamran*' had given him a certificate and he was taking the child to the hospital for injections.

By the seventh injection, the child became completely emaciated.

'*Accha, 'nne kuthi vakkandaa …*' (Father, I don't want to be injected …)

His pleas fell on deaf ears … Keeran would pick up the child at the appointed time and begin to walk like a mail-runner sets out with his swag of letters.

11 injections later, the body of the child bloated and his skin discoloured and became unsightly. At that stage the doctor put a stop to the injections.

'Don't bring the child for some time now,' the doctor ordered Keeran. Keeran's face fell. He picked up the child and trudged back to his hut.

The next morning Keeran found Chathan lying unconscious on the mat. All that came from him was a pathetic whimper.

'*Mone, mone, Chathuttye …*' Keeran called out, seized with pity. (My son, Chathan darling …)

There was no motion. A little later, that whimper also stopped.

Frightened, Keeran called his *cherumi*. All he heard in reply was the feeble wail of a newborn.

Keeran ran outside like a mad dog.

The Offering
Upaharam

It was a clear evening. I dressed up and stepped out of my hotel. The streets of Rome seemed unusually crowded. Ladies and gents in fashionable clothes and sprightly youngsters jostled one another on the pavement. The sun that trickled through the colourful tops of the trees of the boulevard seemed to embrace the life forms below, blessing them.

I approached a bus stop. A bus for tourists that circumambulates the city of Rome was just reaching its shelter. Recalling that the tomb of the English poet Shelley was along the route of the bus marked 'M.D.', I hopped on.

The bus conductor opened his ticket book and gestured to me: 'Where to?'

'*Chimmatheri*,' I said, handing him the money.

Seated in the bus, seeing and enjoying the rows of faded museums replete with beautiful art forms, the walkways resplendent with flowering trees obscuring them, gardens which seemed to smile at the statues in white marble who gesture to the life coursing around them: 'Stop!'—I did not realize the passage of time.

The conductor tapped me on the shoulder and said, '*Cimitero*!'

I got off.

I had reached a huge seemingly endless wall. I walked towards the entrance of that magnificent cemetery. There was a vast courtyard. Along the courtyard sat young girls selling large heaps of flowers.

'Fresh flowers for the tomb of your loved ones,' smiled a pretty little girl touching her basket of flowers.

The freshness of those flowers, the girl's bewitching smile and my love for Shelley persuaded me to buy a bouquet of flowers.

'A small one ...' I said, reaching out.

She dipped into her basket of flowers, picked a small bouquet soaked in water, shook it once and handed it to me.

'Price?'

'150 lira.'

I walked towards the entrance holding the bouquet, guarded by a man in military uniform.

'Can you tell me where the tomb of the English poet Shelley is?'

As if he hadn't understood what I said, he answered me with another question: 'Are you Indian?'

I nodded.

'I have also lived in India—during the war,' his smile held the pride of great achievement. Having seen many Italian prisoners of war who had lived in India, the novelty of it was lost on me.

All I felt was sympathy for this man in khakhi who stood guard at the detention camp of the dead. Still, I said with a smile: 'Oh! Delighted! Can you please tell me where the tomb of the English poet Shelley is?' I repeated the question.

He thought for a while. Then he shook his head and said: 'That isn't here. It is in the Protestant cemetery—a long way off.'

My spirits sank. I stood there despairingly holding that soggy bouquet. I thought I could catch the next bus to go there, but it occurred to me that by dusk, the cemetery would be closed. I stood there for a while not knowing what to do.

Men and women walked past with gloomy expressions, holding flower garlands and bouquets to be placed on the tombs of their loved ones. I looked inside through the entrance gate.

A vast and peaceful cemetery lured me in. A nuptial parlour thrown open by Death itself! I entered slowly, bouquet in hand. When I stepped into the fortress of the final resting place of the citizens of Rome, I felt I was slipping away from life. People moved about like abstract shadows. Often were seen quiet movements of the flowering trees which stood casting their shadows on the tombs; no sobs ... just sighs.

Scores of tombs stretched out in formation with no end in sight; crosses stood conspicuously over them like the symbols which terminated lives. Next to the marble slabs could be seen those of laterite. The poor resting by the lords. Over the marble tombstones on which were etched names and titles, encroached the shadows of wooden crosses which stood guard over the unsung dead. Next to an innocent virgin might repose a ruthless butcher. Overall, what went on there was a shadow puppetry of the enigma of life.

Multitudes came with flower garlands to revive their memories on the anniversaries of the dead. A son to see his father; a father to see his son; a lover to look at his lost love and heave a deep sigh; a girl to shed tears for her departed lover; a wife to offer gifts of love to her husband; an aged husband to surrender his heart to the loving care of his wife.

The silent conflict of myriad emotions.

I was standing beneath a poplar tree observing everything, still holding my bouquet, unable to make up my mind where to place it.

Holding a large bunch of flowers close to her chest, an elderly woman entered with her husband in tow, who walked leaning on a walking stick. They walked slowly towards the poplar tree. The old man had a new toy—a silver aeroplane.

They approached a small tomb. Around the slab of that tomb had been grown flowering climbers. The old woman put down the bunch of flowers and wiped the slab. The old man collected all the dry leaves and wilted flowers around the tomb and threw them away.

The lady placed the bunch of flowers on the tomb and caressed the slab as if she were stroking a sleeping child. The old man wound up the toy plane and put it down, setting it in motion to run around the tomb with a whirring sound. The old man smiled, satisfied. He placed the toy among the creepers and got up.

'Cheeko, *buona notte!'* (Cheeko, goodnight!). With that, the old man turned and moved on.

'Cheeko, *buona notte.'*That old woman too said goodnight.

With neither tears, sobs nor sighs, the old couple walked away.

When they were out of sight, I walked up to that grave and looked at the inscription on the tomb:

Cheeko Pisani

Born: 1906

Died: 1915

That old couple had come to visit the sleeping chamber of their son who had died 35 years ago. They probably believed that their nine-year-old son was still fast asleep. It did not occur to them that if he had lived, he would have been forty-four, a middle-aged man. Even so, to them Cheeko was a little child who craved new toys.

To Death, which had immortalized the childhood of Cheeko, I dedicated my bouquet.

The Story of the Timepiece

Timepieceinte Katha

Four days ago I rented an old house to write my next novel. The house was situated at the center of a large estate in northern Wayanad. It was an old derelict bungalow. It could be said that more than the facilities that the bungalow offered, it was the beauty and tranquility of its surroundings that tempted me to stay there for a spell. That crumbling old bungalow stood atop a huge reddish hill that bordered a creek whose banks were embroidered with verdant jungles. At the southern corner of the hill lay green-pleated tea gardens shaded by silver oak trees. Far west, the stepped grasslands lay resting their heads on the lap of the horizon that pierced the bluish void weighing down on the place. Seated in my room in the northern part of the house I would raise my head often to look up at that colourful and novel scenery, as I worked on the fourth chapter of my novel.

The heroine of the story, Anandalakshmi, had entered the garden of Sudhakara Menon, the hero, and stood with her hand poised to pluck a chempaka flower. Menon was inside shaving. '*The dog of the hero, Churchill, broke its chain ...*'—that is where I had reached. Churchill must run up to Anandalakshmi, pounce on her, bite her and push her to the ground, upon which Sudhakara Menon would run out, his face still covered with lather, and separate the two. Then would begin the blossom of love. That is how I had written the plot.

I began to write: *Anandalakshmi raised her forearm that looked like the stalk of a bamboo, fluttered her eyelids looking all around …*

'Does the dog bite?'

It was not the question from a character in my story. Someone was shouting from the gate of the bungalow.

I put my pen down and went to the verandah. A short old man in a black woollen coat stood at the gate nervously. He had wound a towel around his head. The *mundu,* a length of coarse material that he wore around his waist reached down only to the middle of his calves. He looked like a '*warrant-sipahee*' and held a yellow envelope. I involuntarily recalled, one by one, the faces of all the fellows who had loaned me money.

'The dog is chained. You can enter.'

I called him to the verandah. Apart from Churchill, the dog in my novel, there was no other.

'Are you the new peon?' he asked me as soon as he stepped onto the verandah.

'I am no peon,' I said looking at him, still suspicious.

'There is a writer staying here. Where is he?'

'Only one man resides here, and that is I.'

'All right. See if this letter is for you.' He held out the envelope.

The addressee was myself. I opened the cover:

Kannur, January '14

Sir,

I request you to search out and return the timepiece stored in a cupboard in the southern room of the 'Wood Bain' bungalow along with the bearer of this letter, butler Kunhikoran. With him are the keys to the room.

—Kunnummal Koloth
Chirutha (sd)
(Owner of Wood Bain Bungalow)

I took the keys from Kunhikoran and opened the southern room. All the old and discarded things of the bungalow were stored there. I opened the almirah, inspected it and found the timepiece on the lowest shelf of the cupboard. A small clock, dusty and blackened all over, its face faded and hands frozen. A piece of trash that even the *kaka* in our villages who goes around yelling, '*Old paper … bottles … jars … anything to trash …?*' would not glance at. I hoisted it with two fingers, and asked the old man, 'Is this it?'

'That's the one, sir … that's the one!' He took it from me as if it were a treasure.

I locked the cupboard and the room and returned the keys to the old man and sat on the parapet of the verandah. The butler also sat next to me. He wrapped the timepiece in a handkerchief and placed it on his lap.

'Why do you cherish it so much?' I asked him.

'Have to send it to London, sir … to London.'

'*To London!*' I opened my eyes wide and my jaw dropped. I asked the old man, 'For repairs, perhaps …?'

'Oom ... huh … hoom,' the old man shook his head, in denial. 'The owner of this timepiece is in London.'

'Is it so expensive?'

'Its owner values it greatly and it is being posted on his request. There is a long story behind it!' Butler Kunhikoran continued, stroking that historical item, 'Do you know how many amusing incidents this timepiece has borne witness to? Ha! How time flies …!'

It wasn't that I did not want to hear the story of the timepiece. But I remembered the incomplete fourth chapter. Sudhakara Menon was still shaving. Anandalakshmi had not yet plucked the flower; the dog was standing stunned baring its fangs, having broken free of his chain. I could not delay any further the coming together of the hero, the heroine and the dog. To do so I had to dispense with the old man right away.

'The alarm bell of this timepiece which I heard 20 years ago, still rings in my ears! How many incidents were triggered off by its ring!' The old man was saying all this to himself, staring into the distance.

Those words tempted me. I decided I must listen to that history. I looked at the man's face; he stared at the blazing sun at the end of the western expanse of land, 'Ho! Sunshine like furnace fire!'

'You can leave after sundown,' I advised the old man with an ulterior motive. He agreed.

With the knack of the aged to tell old tales, here is the story that butler Kunhikoran narrated:

'Twenty years ago … the manager of a company called 'P—' was a Scottish gentleman called McCarthy. A tall lean man who looked like a rafter made of jack wood. Around forty years old. He was unmarried. Very different from the usual Englishman, was this McCarthy '*sayvu*'. The conceit, extravagance and the lordly attitude common among his peers had not touched him. He had cultivated a temperament of, '*poda—po*' towards the Britishers in India. It would seem that he was hostile to them. Never going to their clubs or attending their parties, he lived alone with his dog Ruby in his bungalow on the estate. The white community in turn ostracized him. McCarthy cared a hoot! Because McCarthy's father was a lord and one of the directors of the company in London, the discontent of the white men did not bother him.

He was an expert in physical exercises. He would pace around his room in a pair of black shorts displaying his powerfully muscled body. His eyes were like liquid ash. His face was narrow with a long thin nose, flat cheeks and a pointed chin; he would take great pains to keep it glowing by shaving twice every day. On the top of that face was a bald pate that looked like an upturned copper vessel with golden curls forming a border that appeared sewed on around it. All of this made McCarthy *sayvu* unforgettable.

He was grateful to his servants in a strange way. He did not hesitate to speak to them affably and freely while sometimes sharing amusements with them. McCarthy's butler, Nanu, was an expert weightlifter. The secret that McCarthy *sayvu* would wrestle with Nanu in the bathroom was widely known through word spread by the peons of the bungalow. Besides all that he would also display some idiosyncrasies. One of them was the 'American Posture.'

As mentioned before, McCarthy had a dog named Ruby. When he walked into his office the black dog with long woolly fur would follow. Sometimes he would come into the room, bolt the door and walk around in all seriousness. Then he would begin work—picking up each item in the room and placing it upside down. Table, chairs, the picture on the wall, the calendar—satisfied that he had missed nothing, he himself would stand on his head! In this yogic posture, everything would seem upright, isn't it? That is the secret and joy of this idiosyncrasy. The first to see this topsy-turvy project was Raman Nair, the peon. Hearing Ruby whining, he rushed into the office room fearing a calamity. The door was latched from inside. He couldn't hear any movement. Not knowing what to do, Raman Nair ran to the head clerk, Krishna Iyer. Krishna Iyer too came running and peeped in through a slit in the door. Seeing Krishna Iyer snigger with his hand over his mouth, the second clerk, Krishna Panickar pushed him aside and also peeked in—Raman Nair followed suit. Soon the whole staff converged and looked through the slit with their palms cupped around their eyes like children peeking through the lens of the bioscope box on the streets, shaking their heads and snickering. After a quarter of an hour, the *sayvu* straightened up from his yogic meditation. He rearranged all the articles in the room in their former state. Then he sat on a chair, lit a cigarette, opened a magazine and began to read. The clerks returned to their seats with cheeks blown with suppressed laughter and sat quietly.

It was a clerk, by name C.V. Menon, who gave a name to this exercise of the *sayvu*—American Posture. Obviously, the Americans who are on the face of the globe diametrically opposite ours, must be standing like that …!

Gradually, the *sayvu* trained his dog to collude with him and stand upside down as he did. As soon as Ruby saw him prepare for the routine, she would stand against a wall and attempt to raise her hind legs in the air, whimpering pathetically.

This way, he earned a nickname: '*Kirukkan Sayvu*'. *Kirukkan Sayvu* often lost his temper. Then he would attack the workers, beat and punch them and throw things around. After a while when his temper died down, he would go take a shave and call all the servants he beat up and gift each with five or ten rupees. Because of this it was usual for the workers to pray again and again: 'May the *Kirukkan Sayvu* beat me up today!' I was one among them. Those days I was working as a '*chokra*' under his butler.

As days passed, news came that McCarthy *sayvu* had disagreed sharply with the directors of his company, and had resigned. It came to be known that he had bought an estate in Wayanad where he planned to live in total freedom.

'That *Kirukkan* will do that and much more!' said peon Raman Nair.

I had secretly decided that I must pilfer some articles from his bungalow before the *sayvu* left the premises. There was a timepiece on the *sayvu*'s table. I had developed an uncontrollable desire to possess it ever since I saw it. The man was chronically forgetful. He was not likely to notice if the timepiece was missing. And if he did find out, when told, 'It fell and broke, Sir,' he would believe it, no questions asked.

The *savyu* may not know how many things he had himself flung about and shattered when his temper peaked. Nanu butler, who knew fully well the behaviour of the white man, had pinched many articles from the bungalow from time to time. I decided to make an attempt like that. But how could I smuggle the thing out? The peon Raman Nair, who guarded the gate, had been given the authority to check anyone he suspected. Not just the bamboo wicker baskets and the vessels of the women, but even the tuck of the cloth around their waists would be checked by that old chap, without any hesitation. He had the eye of a jackal. Though I foresaw several obstacles, I could not wipe out the greed in my mind to somehow acquire that cute timepiece and smuggle it outside. Considering many ideas, I finally arrived at a strategy.

In the company's department for dispatching coconut fibre ropes, there were many women on wages who spun the fibre into ropes, bundled them and did other things as well. Among them was a certain Matha, a young girl who lived in a small thatched hut near my house. She was like a plump ripe plantain fruit and had no one except an old wizened mother and a little brother. That family survived on the wages she earned.

I requested Matha to help me. At first, she refused.

'Too dangerous. Find someone else!' Though she tried saying all this, finally I got the better of her.

The arrangement was that I would filch the timepiece from the bungalow and hand it over to Matha. She would somehow smuggle it out of the premises.

At 3 o'clock while the *sayvu* was sleeping, I took the timepiece, went to the back of the office building and passed it on to Matha who was waiting among the bushes there. At first she hid it in her basket. Then, fearing its discovery, she tucked it under her jumper, knotted it tight and threw a shawl over it; then she stood waiting for the bell that announced the end of the shift at the factory.

Looking at her face, even a seasoned psychiatrist couldn't tell what a cunning girl she really was—nor did her bosom reveal that she had hidden even a needle in it.

It was routine to let all the women workers leave the premises before 5:30. A lot of shoving and pushing went on at the gate when they did. Raman Nair's inspection commands could be heard intermittently: 'Stop right there, let me see what is bulging in your basket ... open your lunchbox ... what is this swelling in the waist of this old woman ...?' So on and so forth. Along with the women who jostled through the sarcasm and checking, Matha too tried to wriggle out with her timepiece.

'*Krnnng—Nnng—Nnng*'—suddenly, a noise rang out from nowhere. The women and the guard looked around perplexed. *Ngg—Ngg*—the sound continued stridently.

Matha crushed her bosom as if to smother the timepiece to death; whatever deadly antics she tried, she could not silence the gadget. When he saw Matha's struggles, Raman Nair's doubts about the source of that sound were confirmed.

Raman Nair picked Matha from among the giggling, jostling women and presented her before McCarthy. Even then the bell continued to ring from inside Matha's blouse. Her heart below it beat faster than the ring of the timepiece.

Matha was partially stripped and the timepiece extricated. At the sight of the timepiece—whose alarm he had set to ring at 5:30—emerging from Matha's bosom, the *sayvu* gawked. Matha—poor thing—covered her face and burst out crying. She did not answer any questions. McCarthy took the timepiece and let Matha off.

That night, McCarthy *sayvu* burst out laughing again and again.

All of us feared that Matha, in her shame and disgrace would hang herself. Nanu butler said that the *sayvu* had written to the police. I relaxed, thinking that at least for the time being I had escaped.

We spent two days watching the developments of the events that would surely follow. But matters concluded in a totally different manner.

McCarthy married Matha!

The wedding was on the day after the *sayvu* quit the company. McCarthy *sayvu* and *Mathamma* went to Ooty for their honeymoon.

After their honeymoon, it is here in this estate that they came to stay. McCarthy, Matha and Ruby the bitch began to live in this very bungalow—Wood Bain.

Sir, it was a most successful marriage—the coming together of the Scottish *kirukkan* and the poor, docile Malayali girl, Matha. She looked after him with love and care. *Sayvu* worshipped her like a goddess.

After six months, on Matha's recommendation, I too arrived here as their butler.

We lived here for 10 years.

In the eleventh year, Matha died of small pox. She never conceived. It is difficult to describe the sorrow of that white man. He lived like a mad man for another year in this bungalow.

All at once a cable arrived from London to say that his father, the lord, had expired and that he must return home right away.

McCathy donated his bungalow and estate to Matha's old mother and brother, bade his last farewell to India and boarded a ship to England. Since then we have had no news of him. Now here comes a letter—to say that the old timepiece must be found and sent to England. This is proof that even after reaching Scotland, the man's madness continues. Anyway, it is not a matter that will cause us any loss; just a timepiece, isn't it? Besides, sir, he was a good boss. Ought we not to show our gratitude? That is why I have come here personally with much difficulty. I will send it to London by the next mail.'

As Kunhikkoran butler concluded his story of the clock, my own timepiece began to scream from inside to announce, '*two o'clock, time for lunch—Nng, Nng, Nng …*'

I served the butler some lime juice and went indoors for lunch. Hearing the sound of a lorry approaching, the butler called out from the verandah: 'Sir, let me go. I can get a ride back on this lorry.'

After lunch and having rested for a while, I resumed work on the fourth chapter of my novel. The characters in the story were in suspended animation— the hero shaving, the girl with her hand raised and the dog standing still, having just broken free. I could not concentrate to complete writing that fib of a story. My thoughts sailed through the lightning in the sky flashing over the stepped western grasslands, to faraway Scotland.

In the countryside of Scotland, among the cragged slate hills stands a huge old mansion. In the garden before it, cloaked in mist, walks a tall, sturdy old man, with a dog at his heels. The mailman walks in and hands over a parcel to him. The old man, excited on seeing an Indian stamp on it, opens the packet and takes out an old timepiece. Like holding a baby who had thrashed about on the bosom of his loving wife, he holds it pressed against his chest. He stands with his head bowed, stroking the bald pate which looks like an upturned copper cauldron. The chime of the bells of old memories! His ashen-grey eyes brim over …

Lost in that daydream, I drifted off into a light sleep.

Farewell!
Quahe-Ri!

I sat lost in thought for a long time after reading the letter I received from Mr Gomez, my friend in Nigeria. It was the last bit of news in it that wrenched my heart: '*Sally was shot dead by white men.*'

My thoughts drifted to the days I had spent in Kenya four years ago. Those days the 'Mumu' organization had not yet taken root; the government had not begun to pay compensation for the heads of the Mumu organizers harvested. The Kikuyu Negroes were living peacefully in towns as domestic servants and in the villages as farmers. But their eyes reflected the dark shadows of discontent and the pain of unjust oppression. Nobody imagined then that those dark shadows would one day billow like a forest fire to smother Kenya completely. Someone had forewarned me sympathetically of an impending revolution. That man was Sally.

When I read Gomez' letter, some of the matters that Sally had told me crept into my mind. 'If all these Kikuyus secretly organize themselves and prepare to revolt, the white man will have no recourse but to cast away his bundle of arrogance and scoot across the seas. There are 40 lakh Negroes and a lakh of Indians in Kenya. What can 27,000 white men do against them?'

'Let no Englishman hope in vain to rule by the gun Negro lands which the missionary Livingstone conquered by love'—these words were spoken by a white man!

His real name was Seles or something. But he was known as 'Sally'.

I first met him on the train from Mombassa to Nairobi. I was having tea in the dining car that evening. A white man sat there with a bottle of beer and a mug before him, looking out through the glass window of the coach at the rugged African terrain outside. That man with copper-coloured hair, blue eyes and a long sharp nose suddenly turned to me and asked in a cracked but sweet voice: 'Are you going to Nairobi?'

'Yes, I'm going to Nairobi,' I said meekly, 'And you?'

'I'm going to Nayeri—will get off at Woi station.'

I had not expected to be addressed by that white man. Even at first glance I felt an instinctive regard for him. In Africa, the behavior of the white man in the presence of a dark-skinned person was generally different. When caught before the blacks, the white man, displaying his 'superior' white skin, would assume a vow of silence. To speak to black people in his native English was a disgrace. If he had to say something to them he would order, not speak, in broken Swahili. But here was an exception! We then spent some time in silence as if there was nothing to be asked or said anymore. He resumed his watch through the window. I also watched the wilderness go by.

The train was meandering through the gorges among barren hills. Rocks dulled by dust, soil the colour of flesh and knolls that looked like horses' manes, cropped up now and then. Baobab trees peeked with bloated tummies. Swollen, curled and wrinkled at places, wild creepers which looked like waves hung along the way. Bramble bushes that looked like the heads of Negroes appeared intermittently. Then could be seen groups of plants which looked like skeletons. From the thorny trees standing alone on the hills hung nests which looked like silken streamers. Sporadic huge anthills stood guard over that desolate void. Those scenes evoked not joy but a kind of gloomy distress.

'Where do you work? In a government office or on the plantations?' he turned to me and asked mildly.

When I told him that I was a traveller who had come to see Africa, his blue eyes widened and with a broad lingering smile, he looked at me, slanting his head.

'Really?' He edged closer to me.

'My name is Sally,' he introduced himself. 'My father is a planter in Nayeri. The prodigal that I am, he has disowned me. I wander around enjoying the native beauty of Africa—that completes my life story.'

(It was much later that I learnt from Gomez that Sally was a graduate from Oxford University and that his father was one of the richest men in Kenya).

I took out a cigarette case from my pocket and proffered the open case to Sally.

'I don't smoke. Haven't acquired minor vices, thank you!' Sally smirked, kissing his beer mug. 'How long have you been in Africa?'

'Six months.'

'In these six months have you been able to see the intrinsic beauty of Africa?'

I sat there staring blankly not knowing what to say. Intrinsic beauty of Africa? What is that?

'Have you ever drunk 'Pompey' liquor? Grey and viscous, frothing, sour Pompey liquor?'

'No.'

'Then you ought to try that local brew. You will hear the pulse of Africa drumming victory marches in your brain.'

'Have you danced with the negroes?'

'No.'

'Try dancing with the 'Goma'—folk dance group—a dance which portrays the craving of man to merge with the forces that control the elements ... you will feel like you are dancing to the heartbeat of Africa.'

'I might experience all that. But I am tired of seeing the wilted shrubs and scorched hills of this place over and over again.'

Sally poured some beer into his mug and said, 'You are seeing only the superficial scenery. That is not enough. Obvious beauty will not have any life in it. The life of beauty is the mysticism intrinsic to it.'

Probably because the signal did not indicate assent, the train stopped on the slope of a hill.

'What a beautiful view!'

'What view?' Apart from some uncouth rocks I saw nothing.

'Over there! Look at that wild plant standing erect in the crevice of the rocks!'

I looked. Near the track among rocks stood a wild plant, as tall as a man—with curved thorny stalks forming a shape like the human ribcage.

'What is so beautiful about it?'

'Concentrate! Can't you see it dance to share joyously the coarse and parched state of nature?'

When I looked with renewed interest, I began to think that what he said was true. That wild plant danced showing expressive mudras in harmony with nature. Reminiscent of a *Nataraja nritham*!

'Look at the tiny flowers that stick to it like gemstones. Have you ever seen similar dainty flowers with such a refreshing colour?'

I looked at the flowers scattered on the bosom of that wild plant. Against the backdrop of black rocks and the dark green faded with dust, glowed dots of bright red! I felt like singing out loud: '*Ithiri Poove, Chukanna Poove* ...'

'Like those red flowers hiding in that wild plant, do you know of the romance that sprouts from the hearts of Negro women?'

I was not prepared to hear Sally go to that extent. A white man in search of love, peeks into the heart of a Negro woman! Might he be speaking from experience?

The train whistled and began to move. Spewing black smoke into the atmosphere that resembled faded paper, it trundled into the jungles.

The golden rays of the setting sun scattered over thorny trees wearing masks of cobwebs. Kikuyu Mountain, the colour of purple, rose with its head held high above a strange ring of ochre which could not be distinguished between the changed colour of the sky and the reign of the smoke.

Looking at my eyes gazing upon the scenes of the African sunset, Sally said: 'The day is about to bid farewell—at the moment of separation, anything will have a special kind of beauty ...'

'You could be right.'

Sally looked at the sun sinking behind the Kikuyu mountains,

'*Quahe-ri* ...'

I did not understand the meaning of what he said. What is it that he said?

Sally asked me: 'When you say goodbye and part, what Indian word do you use?'

I tried to recall—we don't have a farewell phrase that can be compressed into a single word. The North Indians say 'Namasthe' or '*Alvidaa.*' '*Ennal anganeyavatte, pinnekkanaam* ...' is the loose manner of saying goodbye of the Malayali. I did not tell Sally all this.

'*Namasthe*—that is what the Indians say when parting formally.' I apprised Sally.

'Namasthe,' Sally tried to pronounce the word. Then shaking his head, he said: '"Namaaste"—"Namaaste" doesn't sound poetic. In English, we say Goodbye or Farewell. They don't sound very earnest, either. Au revoir—what the French say on parting—is a lot more evocative. But of all the words of farewell that I have heard, the most musical, heart rending and sweetly simple is in the language of the Negroes—*Quahe-ri*.'

Tipping the remaining beer in the bottle into the mug and tilting his head to the bottle, he pronounced that word once more, sweetly: '*Quahe-ri*.'

Bidding farewell to the last drop in his mug, Sally said: '*Quahe-ri*.'

'In the literature of faith, if ever a poem is written in a single word, this is it—*Quahe-ri*. It is the poem that ensnared me in love: *Quahe-ri*.'

The moment when even our best friends become boring is when they unwrap the book of their adventures in love before us. But I couldn't contain my eagerness to hear Sally's love story. I realized that he was about to tell me about it even without persuasion. Sally had ordered a fresh bottle of beer.

Outside the window, the light of the setting sun had begun to fade. We could see dimly the populated slopes of the hills. Kikuyus were droving their cattle back to their hamlets. Their huts could be seen at a distance like pointed caps arranged in rows.

'I'm going to tell you that story ...' Sally said, looking with angst at the distant village of the Kikuyus.

I shall recount that story here as Sally related it:

'It was a time when I had taken a fancy to research the dance forms of Africa. Many allegations spread in my own white community that I was cohabiting with the Negroes excessively.

I neither regretted my work nor did I confront my critics. Because, I knew that I was more simple and honest than the other members of my society. I would go to the villages of the Negroes and join them in their dances and often sleep overnight in their huts. My endeavour was to assimilate everything about their dances.

Gradually I was able to meld with the lifestyle of the Negroes and discovered that sincerity, love and a disposition to help each other were pronounced traits in their etiquette. As I progressed this way, I began to grow distant from my own community. Finally, my father disowned me. I packed up and went to Nayeri to study the Kikuyus more deeply.

I stayed in a small village there for a month. A section of their community became suspicious of me. They were convinced that I was an '*anjampathikkaran*'. An occultist, the brother-in-law of the village chieftain and a hunchbacked Kikuyu—a fellow who had served a jail sentence of four years for having stolen a white man's dog, slaughtered it and made 'chops-curry' of it—became my sworn enemies. The occultist feared that the '*Musoongu*' (white man) might lay bare his secrets. The chieftain's brother-in-law was jealous of the love and respect that the chief showed me. The jailbird, that hunchback Kikuyu, had an inherent hatred of all white men.

I ignored their animosity. I participated in their dances at night and spent days inside the hut making figurines with plaster of Paris, depicting the postures and symbols portrayed in their dance forms. The village chief had made a hut especially for me to live in.

One night, asleep on the bamboo cot inside the hut, I was startled awake by a loud whisper, '*Bwana, bwana*!' Frightened, I found my flashlight and switched it on. There stood at the foot of my bed, a Negro girl!

I asked her, a little cross: 'Who are you? What do you want?'

'*Bwana*, a dark panther is going to attack you—your foot will be bitten by the panther. It will swell and you will die. Escape quickly. I have said what I must. I am off now.'

Her form withdrew from the hut and vanished into the thickets outside. I rubbed my eyes and looked around, to make sure it wasn't a dream. It wasn't. I had seen that girl before among the dancers frequently. She had often smiled at me. Now, here she comes at this odd hour to warn me and vanishes!

I felt what she said must be seriously thought over. The Negroes would go to any extent for revenge. My heart whispered to me that something amiss was going to take place in the hut that night. I had heard quite a lot about the predatory techniques of the Negroes. Didn't she say I would die of a swollen foot? I knew that scheme. I grinned to myself, determined to watch the panther bite my foot.

I couldn't let my foot be bitten by a black panther, could I? An idea occurred to me spontaneously. I positioned two white legs made of soft plaster at the foot of the bed where my own feet might have been and lay there motionless, all covered up, legs tucked in. I had my revolver with me. I have no idea how long I remained like that.

I heard the bamboo door of the hut creak. My eyes darted to the door. Someone had left the door open. The light of the night sky peeped into the room. In the dim light, I saw a black figure creeping towards my cot—black panther!

For a long moment, the black form stayed at the foot of my bed, completely silent. Then it returned. The door was seen closed once more, as before. After waiting for a long while, I got up and inspected the feet of plaster. There was a black spot on the underside of the heel of the left foot! There was also the mark of a needle prick.

I realized that a caustic venom had been injected into that foot. It might have entered my own foot! I knew that the 'black panther' was the venerable occultist covered in leopard skin. I could have shot dead the bloke even at first sight. But I did not do so.

I decided to bid farewell to that village the next day. In my desire to see the girl who had saved my life, I went to each hutment on the pretext of saying goodbye. But to no avail. Depressed, I walked with my box along the forest path that led to the road.

'*Jambo, Bwana*!'

From behind the outcrop of rocks by the side of the path floated a greeting in a soft voice. I turned my head to look. There she was! Standing behind a tall wild plant with flowers tinged crimson, she raised her hand and waved, exposing teeth like studded diamonds, spreading the brilliance of her beautiful smile—'*Quahe-ri*'.

I offered many precious articles in my box to her. She merely stood there shaking her head, refusing to take any of them. Finally I asked her, 'What is your name?'

'Kabeena,' she said, casting her eyes downward.

'Which is your hut? I looked for you all around but couldn't find you.'

'I live in Mukuru's hut. I am his daughter.'

I was taken aback. Mukuru was the name of the occultist! I again tried to gift her something from my box—no go. She declined all of them, shaking her head with that diamond-studded smile of hers.

Dejected, I moved on, leaving her standing there. When I looked back, she was standing behind that plant; she waved, calling out, '*Quahe-ri* …'

That evening, I boarded a train for Mombasa. My thoughts were full of her during the ride. Those crimson flowers, the black rock, that brilliant smile and black Kabeena—all together kept churning in my mind.

'*Quahe-ri* …' That melody continued to dive deep and swim at the bottom of my heart.

'Why didn't she accept anything from me?' I couldn't figure that out, much as I thought over it. At last realization struck me as the train stopped at Tsavo station—what Kabeena wanted was my love!

I did not go to Mombasa; I got off at Tsavo. The next day I went back to Nayeri. I married Kabeena. Yes, I am the son-in-law of a Negro occultist—I am going to my wife's house …'

Sally got off at Woi station. Carrying his large leather case in one hand and smiling, Sally raised his hand and said to me: '*Quahe-ri*!'

I responded with a mixture of love and respect: '*Quahe-ri*!'

In the dim light of Woi railway station, Sally walked out, amidst many Negroes through the 'Exit for Residents', and vanished.

Till I reached Nairobi, my thoughts revolved around that white man who had blended with a Negro clan. The joy and gratitude of having met a good man in my African travels, rippled in my heart.

Next I heard of Sally was through the letter from Gomez of Nairobi. Not very detailed; just one sentence: '*Sally was shot dead by white men.*'

The world will never know the story of a revolutionary that lies hidden in that sentence.

'Sally, *Quahe-ri* …'

Glossary

aapu chaya. 'Half tea', as spoken by an illiterate Malayali villager.
Achan. A Malayalam word for father.
Adhikari Thamran. Master, landlord.
Aikya Keralam. United Keralam.
Akka. Elder sister—used as a form of address.
Ammae. '*Amma*' means mother. The word is inflected to *Ammae* when a mother is addressed in Malayalam.
amsam adhikari. Village headman.
ana. A denomination of currency of the time; sixteen anas made a rupee.
aniyara. A green room where the characters in a play adorn themselves.
anjampathikkaran. Traitor.
Anna. *Anna*, or elder brother, is used as a suffix in a name to convey respect for an older person.
aripoo and ***odichukuthipoo***. Local names of flowers in Malayalam.
arippa chedi and ***thechi maram***. Species of Chrysanthus.
attamkazha. A pole and makeshift bucket to lift water from irrigation furrows in paddy fields.
ayanippilavu. A jackfruit tree.
ayasanigadam. Iron vice.

balapankthi. Children's section.
Bappa. Urdu term for father.
becha. A cycle-rickshaw.
beedi. A small upcountry cheroot made of tobacco leaves rolled up tightly.
betel concoction. Araca nut and lime wrapped in betel leaf and chewed as a concoction.
Bha! An outburst, a meaningless expletive showing utmost contempt.
Bhadrakali. The goddess of devastation
Bhagavat Geetha. A treatise on life and living from the epic *Mahabharata*.
bundar. Harbour.

Chada, Pada. This is used here by the author to describe a thumping sound, presumably of someone hurrying down the stairs.
chaya. Malayalam for tea.
cheenabharani. Chinese cistern.
chempaka. Botanical name *Michelia champaca*. A flowering tree with a heady scent widely used to decorate long hair.
cherumi. A low-caste woman who works the fields owned by landlords along with her husband, a *cheruman*.

chimmatheri. Pronunciation of the Italian word *cimitero*, meaning cemetery, written in Malayalam in the original.
chokra. An odd-jobs boy.
chootu. A torch made by bundling dry leaves of palm together and lighting one end.
chudalamada. An invective implying a lowly born person.
CID. A detective from the Central Intelligence Department.
comrade. A Communist sympathizer.
Coorg. A verdant district that shares its borders with Karnataka and Kerala, whose people speak a pidgin with its elements taken from the languages of both states.
Cuticura powder. Cuticura used to be a very popular, strongly scented talc of the time.

eenthalchacka. A date fruit.
Elappa. Father's younger brother; term used in a Muslim dialect.
elathalam. Cymbals used as accompaniment for temple drums.
elephant door. A tall door large enough to let an elephant pass through it; also indicative of the house of a feudal landlord.
Ennal anganeyavatte, pinnekkanaam. 'So be it, see you later'
ettameen. A variety of fish.

flags. Penalty points.

godown. Term used for warehouse in India and eastern Asia.
granthavarikal. Chronicles recorded and preserved in palaces and temples.

Hajiyar. The title of a person who has undertaken the pilgrimage to Mecca (Haj).
hasyanatakam. Parody.
hoorling. A celestial nymph.

ICS. Indian Civil Service.
Idavapathi. The month straddling June and July, months of torrential rains in Kerala.
ilanji. A flower with a pleasant, strong smell, often worn by girls in their hair.
Ithiri Poove, Chukanna Poove. 'Little flower, red flower …'—a folk song sung during Onam festival.

Jari-puranawalas. The tribe of collectors of old articles who ply their trade on the streets.

Kaka. A form of address for elder brothers among Muslims.
Kamashasthram. The science of sexual intercourse.
kammati. A hardwood tree.
kammati maram. A kind of tree growing in the wilderness.
kanakamalyam. Golden flower garland. Suggestive of the all-pervasive flowering of plants during the Onam season.
karanavar. The head of the family.

Karkidakam. A month of rains.
Kaveri Sankramam. A festival to worship the river Kaveri for the gift of its waters.
Keechakan. A character in the Mahabharata who is the epitome of debauchery and strength.
Keraleeyar. The people of Keralam.
khadar. A cloth of coarse texture usually made in a handloom, worn by politicians, intellectuals and thinkers to mark renunciation of the material world.
Kikuyu. A tribe in Mount Kenya forming 22 per cent of Kenya's population.
Kirukkan Sayvu. Crazy white man.
kolambi. A spittoon. In the story, it is a sarcastic reference to the cup-like flash unit of the old-world camera that resembled a spittoon.
konakam. Thong; a loin cloth.
Kuberan. The God of wealth, personified here.
Kunhetta. Form of addressing the elder brother.
kunni. A climber, creeper.
Kurathipattu. Kurathi is a woman of the nomadic tribes of soothsayers who sing melodious songs for alms.
kurikalyanam. A wedding feast held for collecting donations.
kuthupala. The dry scoop-shaped spathe of the araca nut leaf.

lathi-charged. Caning for law enforcement; used to disperse crowds.
lungi. A printed sarong worn in Keralam.

machi. A barren woman.
mada. Den
Madanan. Madanan is a character in Malayalam literature who epitomizes the spurned lover.
Madhurolya, Embrane. 'No sugar, my lord!' The language used is the distorted Malayalam of the illiterate low-caste farm labourer.
Malabar. Malabar is the northern provinces of Kerala, put together.
Malay. People inhabiting the lands of Malaysia and Indonesia.
Malayalanadu. Keralam, the land of Malayalam.
Malayali. Belonging to Keralam, speaking the native language Malayalam.
manakal. The plural of *mana*— the word used by the author here; it means house in Kannada, the language of Karnataka.
manda. Derogatory slang for head.
Manjari. A Dravidian metre (music).
manthram. A magic spell.
Mappila. Refers to Muslims of Arab descent domiciled in Kerala through generations. Its literal meaning, therefore, is 'son-in-law'.
Mathrubhoomi Azhchapathippu. *Mathrubhoomi* is a renowned publishing house in Kerala which publishes periodicals and books. *Azhchapathippu* is the Malayalam term for weekly.
Mercara. The anglicized name of Coorg's main township.
Mithunam. A Malayalam month that partially straddles the months of June and July.
mudras. Symbols used in Indian dance forms.

Mumu. An organization of local communities against poverty.
***musumbi* juice.** Orange juice.

Namaskaram! Greetings!
nandyarvattam. A nondescript plant with white flowers without any fragrance.
Narasimhan. Narasimhan is the most ferocious incarnation of Vishnu, where he assumes the form of half-human and half-lion to annihilate the demon, Hiranyakashipu.
Nataraja nritham. Nataraja is Lord Siva; *nritham* is dance. *Nataraja nritham* is 'the dance of the apocalypse'.
nirmalyam. The residue of floral offerings made to the deity the previous day.
nishagandhi. A flower that spreads fragrance in the night.

Onam. The harvest festival of Kerala.
Onappattu. Song sung during the festival of Onam. The one mentioned in the story is a folk song describing the planting of trees on hills.
Onathallu. During the festival of Onam, there is a fun-filled ritual of beating each other up, called *Onathallu*.
ottakurukkan. A lone jackal.

paalakkolu. Wilted spathe of the araca tree.
padipura. Gatehouse.
Palani Ponmalakku Hara Haro Hara. The chorus of prayer seeking the blessing of Lord Murugan of the Palani Hills. This is the chant of the pilgrims on their journey to the Palani Hills.
Panchavati. Panchavati is a verdant cottage built in the forest where Rama stayed during his exile in the *Ramayana*.
parda. The loose over-garment worn by devout Muslim women to thwart unwanted male attention.
pathiri. A pancake.
Pattar. Malayalam slang for Brahmin.
peepavandi. Barrel-mounted cart.
poda—po. An 'Oh, push off' attitude.
Poove, Poli Poove. A popular song sung during the plucking of flowers in the Onam season.
Prabhe. In the Malayali form of address the name Prabha becomes Prabhe, and *Achan* becomes *Acha*.
pulakkalli maram. A forest tree.
pulayadiyanthiram. The ritual performed after a specific term after death.
pullu. A bird of omen.
Puthari. The day after paddy harvest.

rasabindu. Like mercury, a fount of impulses.

Samajam. Usually the Kerala Samajam, a community formed by the people of Kerala living outside the state.
samaram. Revolt.
satyagrahi. A person who pickets for his rights.

sayvu. A Malayalam slang for white men; originally 'sahib' or master.
Seethadevi. Sita of the *Ramayana*.
ser. A measure of rice equal to about a kilogram.
Shashti Poorthy. Sixtieth birthday, celebrated with family and friends who seek the blessings of the birthday boy.
Shoorpanakha. A female demon who, in disguise, tried to entice Rama, but whose nose and breasts were cut off by Rama's brother, Lakshman.
Shornur. A place in central Kerala.

thadaka. A female demon of Indian mythology.
Thalapoli. A ritual when unmarried girls stand in a row carrying platters with flowers and a burning wick on it during temple festivals to welcome the deity.
thanki. Little sister.
tharavad. Ancestral home.
tharavaditham. Aristocracy.
thatha. The Muslim term for elder sister.
thechi. A common flowering plant in Kerala.
theevandi. *Theevandi* literally means 'fire vehicle', alluding to a steam locomotive. These were prevalent at the time of the story.
thilakam. A dot of vermillion worn on the forehead by women to augment their beauty.
Third Class. There were three classes of travel on trains those days: First, Second and Third Class, the last being the cattle class.
Thiruvathira Njatthuvela. The period after mid-June ideal for transplanting paddy, seedlings.
thorth mundu. A coarse absorbent bathing towel used in Kerala.
Thullalpattu and ***Aattakathakal***. These are two temple art forms of Keralam performed during festivals which include both satire and the rendition of epic tales.

unnuka. A Malayalam word that means to have a meal of rice and curry mashed together.
Uppa. Father.

Vaikunth. The abode of Vishnu, the final destination of the soul. The author suggests here the similarity of normal sleep to the eternal.
vermilion. A pigment smeared along the parted hairline of a bride's forehead by the groom to mark the bond of marriage.
veshti. A soft folded linen draped over one shoulder to signify social stature.
Vilasalatika, Nalini, Leela. The three names are of ballads of love written by revered poets of Kerala.

warrant-sipahee. An employee of the court assigned to hand-deliver warrants.
Wayanad. The high range of northern Kerala.

Yakshisamrajyam. The domain of celestial blood-sucking temptresses who lure their victims with their beauty.
yawed. Yaw (nautical): the movement of a boat about its vertical axis.